"So you have never been in love,"
the _Duc_ said.

Startled, Lina looked down, trying to avoid his eyes that seemed to reach down into her soul.

"When one is really in love," he continued, "one becomes part of the person one loves. Then there are no divisions, no barriers! Love is overwhelming and completely absorbing."

"Not everybody experiences the love you are talking about!" said Lina. "It may be very different from what I mean by it."

"I doubt if there is any difference," the _Duc_ answered, "but it might be definitely exciting to find out."

Books by Barbara Cartland

THE ADVENTURER
AGAIN THIS RAPTURE
ARMOUR AGAINST LOVE
THE AUDACIOUS ADVENTURESS
BARBARA CARTLAND'S BOOK OF BEAUTY
    AND HEALTH
THE BITTER WINDS OF LOVE
BLUE HEATHER
BROKEN BARRIERS
THE CAPTIVE HEART
THE COIN OF LOVE
THE COMPLACENT WIFE
COUNT THE STARS
CUPID RIDES PILLION
DANCE ON MY HEART
DESIRE OF THE HEART
DESPERATE DEFIANCE
THE DREAM WITHIN
A DUEL OF HEARTS
ELIZABETH EMPRESS OF AUSTRIA
ELIZABETH IN LOVE
THE ENCHANTED MOMENT
THE ENCHANTED WALTZ
THE ENCHANTING EVIL
ESCAPE FROM PASSION
A GHOST IN MONTE CARLO
THE GOLDEN GONDOLA
A HALO FOR THE DEVIL
A HAZARD OF HEARTS
A HEART IS BROKEN
THE HEART OF THE CLAN
THE HIDDEN EVIL
THE HIDDEN HEART
THE HORIZONS OF LOVE
IN THE ARMS OF LOVE
THE IRRESISTIBLE BUCK
JOSEPHINE EMPRESS OF FRANCE
THE KISS OF THE DEVIL
THE KISS OF PARIS
A KISS OF SILK
THE KNAVE OF HEARTS
THE LEAPING FLAME
A LIGHT TO THE HEART
LIGHTS OF LOVE
THE LITTLE PRETENDER
LOST ENCHANTMENT
LOST LOVE
LOVE AND LINDA
LOVE FORBIDDEN
LOVE AT FORTY
LOVE HOLDS THE CARDS

LOVE IN HIDING
LOVE IN PITY
LOVE IS AN EAGLE
LOVE IS CONTRABAND
LOVE IS DANGEROUS
LOVE IS THE ENEMY
LOVE IS MINE
LOVE ME FOREVER
LOVE TO THE RESCUE
LOVE ON THE RUN
LOVE UNDER FIRE
THE MAGIC OF HONEY
MESSENGER OF LOVE
METTERNICH THE PASSIONATE
    DIPLOMAT
MONEY, MAGIC AND MARRIAGE
NO HEART IS FREE
THE ODIOUS DUKE
OPEN WINGS
OUT OF REACH
PASSIONATE PILGRIM
THE PRETTY HORSE-BREAKERS
THE PRICE IS LOVE
A RAINBOW TO HEAVEN
THE RELUCTANT BRIDE
THE RUNAWAY HEART
THE SCANDALOUS LIFE OF KING
    CAROL
THE SECRET FEAR
THE SMUGGLED HEART
A SONG OF LOVE
STARS IN MY HEART
STOLEN HALO
SWEET ADVENTURE
SWEET ENCHANTRESS
SWEET PUNISHMENT
THEFT OF A HEART
THE THIEF OF LOVE
THIS TIME IT'S LOVE
TOUCH A STAR
TOWARDS THE STARS
THE UNKNOWN HEART
THE UNPREDICTABLE BRIDE
A VIRGIN IN MAYFAIR
A VIRGIN IN PARIS
WE DANCED ALL NIGHT
WHERE IS LOVE?
THE WINGS OF ECSTASY
THE WINGS OF LOVE
WINGS ON MY HEART
WOMAN THE ENIGMA

BARBARA CARTLAND

92

TOUCH A STAR

A JOVE BOOK

First Jove edition published October 1981

First printing

Printed in the United States of America

Jove books are published by Jove Publications, Inc.,
200 Madison Avenue, New York, N.Y. 10016

It was the Russian Arch-Dukes who at the end of the last century started to give fantastically expensive parties in Europe.

Their wild extravagance started in Russia with Nicholas I who believed that power was best demonstrated by splendour. He would employ thousands of workmen to transform gardens into oriental palaces or ballrooms into gardens complete with rockeries and foundations.

Fabulously wealthy noblemen sent their bailiffs to Dresden or Sevres to purchase 500-piece dinner services, which were laboriously carried to Russia by wagon, only after a gargantuan feast, to be used as a shooting target.

The Royal Dukes behaved with spectacular excess in Paris and Baden Baden, decking their favourite *poule de luxe* with jewels and if she visited Russia, decorating her sleighs with emeralds.

The French had already been educated in extravagance by the Courtesans of the Second Empire. Cora

Pearl, an Englishwoman, had jewels worth a million francs and gave suppers at which the peaches and grapes rested on fifteen hundred francs' worth of Parma violets. She danced on a floor strewn with a vanload of exotic orchids and one of her lovers sent her a massive silver horse filled with jewels and gold.

Chapter One

WALKING HOME through the woods Lady Lina Cressington-Combe was humming a tune to herself.

It was a sunny day in early April, the buds were just bursting green on the bushes, and the first snowdrops were pushing through the leaves under the trees.

Lina felt happy, and for the moment she forgot all her difficulties at the Castle and had no wish to remember there were a dozen things waiting for her to do once she returned.

She had escaped after breakfast, her father being in one of his bad moods because he had drunk too much the night before.

Ever since her mother had died two years ago he had consoled himself for his loss by drinking and gambling.

The former, Lina had told him often enough, was ruining his health, while it was impossible for them to afford any losses at the card-tables.

"Please, Papa, be sensible!" she had pleaded with him, not once, but a thousand times.

1

When he was in a good mood he promised her that he would neither go to London, which invariably ended in financial disaster at the tables, nor spend his time when he was at the Castle with Sir Hector Standish.

Lina hated Sir Hector.

He was not only a bad influence on her father, but he was pursuing her in a manner which she had begun to find not only embarrassing, but positively menacing.

A widower for the last ten years, he had been quite content with his bachelor existence until six months ago when he had noticed her for the first time.

Before that she had just been a child whom he patted on the head when he visited her father and occasionally remembered to bring her some peaches from his greenhouses or a box of chocolates.

These, she was well aware, were in those days, not a compliment to herself but simply the consequence of his being snobby enough to appreciate that an Earl, even an impoverished one, was of some consequence amongst those with whom he habitually associated.

Sir Hector had inherited his Baronetcy from his father who had earned it in trade and was therefore not accepted by the County families.

When his father died Sir Hector was determined that because he had been to a Public School and was an exceedingly rich man he should be acknowledged by those who had previously shown him a "cold shoulder."

Two months ago he had suddenly become aware that a ticket to the position he wished to occupy lay in the hands of the young and, as he now realised, beautiful daughter of the man he considered his closest friend.

When he proposed to Lina she had stared at him incredulously, thinking she could not have heard him aright.

At forty she considered Sir Hector an old man, a contemporary of her father, and it had never crossed her mind that he might be one of the suitors her mother had predicted would one day surround her.

"You are going to be very lovely, my darling," she had said when Lina celebrated her sixteenth birthday, "and I pray that your father and I will be able to afford to give you a Ball."

The Countess had sighed.

"I am afraid it will not be as grand as the Ball I had when I came out, but nevertheless the Baronial Dining-Room looks very attractive by candlelight, and once you are launched I am certain that a lot of other people will invite you to their Balls."

"I am sure they will, Mama," Lina smiled, "but you must get well first. Then we can start saving."

But her mother had grown weaker and weaker until finally at the end of the year she had died, and to Lina it was as if the light had left the Castle and there was nothing but darkness and debts.

"I would rather starve than marry Sir Hector!" she told herself after he had proposed.

Then she shuddered in apprehension since it was obvious he was going to be very persistent and would not take 'no' for an answer.

He was now riding over from his large and ostentatious newly-built house almost every day.

He brought her gifts which she longed to refuse, but knew it would annoy her father.

"Standish is a damned good friend, and make no mistake about it!" he said when Lina protested that he came too often.

"I do not like him, Papa."

"Well, I find him useful," the Earl said firmly.

Lina looked at her father apprehensively.

"What do you mean by that, Papa? Are you borrowing money from him? Oh, please, do not do that!"

"I will not have you interfering," the Earl replied.

But he would not meet her eyes, and Lina was certain that the money that paid for the few servants they had left and which met the more pressing tradesmen's bills came from a source which her father would not mention, but was not the Bank.

She did not tell her father that Sir Hector had proposed, and she was almost sure that he was unaware of his "friend's" interest in her.

She thought, although she was not sure, that Sir Hector, aware of the vast discrepancy in their age was afraid that the Earl would laugh at him for having such pretensions, and this, Lina thought, was her one safeguard.

At the same time she had been aware that this last month her father's financial position was worsening even though he would not discuss it.

If she asked him for money for the wages and for the local tradesmen he waved her off with promises

4

of "tomorrow," "next week," "the end of the month."

But she knew when almost every night he went to The Towers for dinner and came back in the early hours of the morning, that he was gambling with the raffish friends with whom Sir Hector filled his house.

She did not need to listen to the local gossip to know they were the hard-riding, hard-drinking neighbours of whom her mother had never approved.

Also there were guests from London who included ladies who would certainly not be acceptable by the hostesses in the County whom Sir Hector always disparaged.

"I know those sour-faced, straight-laced old crows do not approve of me," he had once said to Lina, "but when we're married it will be different. The Towers needs a mistress with class, and that's what you will give it once you're living there."

Young and unsophisticated though she was, Lina understood that he was wooing her not only for herself, although that was frightening enough, but because she was her mother and father's daughter.

There was nobody in the whole County who had not loved her mother, and that her family was as blue-blooded, if not more so, as the Wallinghams had been appreciated by those who would not permit Sir Hector Standish and his friends to cross their thresholds.

"We must draw the line somewhere," Lina had heard the Duchess of Dorset say to her mother, "and however much he may contribute to the Hunt or to our Charities, I have made it quite clear to my husband that I will not entertain that common, red-faced man."

5

Her mother had agreed, although not so vehemently. She was too gentle to be rude or unkind to anybody.

But she had made sure that Sir Hector was not included in the few dinner-parties they gave, and it was only after her death that he had moved in to console her father and then it was impossible to keep him out.

Yesterday, Lina remembered, Sir Hector had been particularly tiresome.

"I intend to marry you, Lina," he said, "and the sooner you make up your mind to accept me, the better!"

"I am sorry, Sir Hector, but you know my answer," Lina replied.

"Good God, girl! Do you not realise what I can give you?" he asked. "You will have gowns from the finest dressmakers in London, jewels that will make every other woman's eyes pop out of her head with envy, and horses that are better bred and more expensive than any other woman in the County has a chance of riding."

"What you must understand, Sir Hector," Lina said quietly, "is that when I marry it will not be for what my husband can give me, but because I love him."

"You're too young to know anything about love," Sir Hector replied, "but I'll teach you to love me."

The way he spoke made Lina shiver.

Looking at his coarse face, red from over-drinking, and the lines of dissipation under his eyes, she noticed that his hair was already grey at the temples.

He was an old man and even to think of being married to him made her feel a revulsion it was hard to hide.

"I know you mean to be kind, Sir Hector," she said, "but please accept as final that I will not marry you, and do not bring me any more presents."

He started to expostulate, almost shouting that she could not escape him, and because she could not bear to listen she ran away.

She only wondered now if instead of running away she should tell her father what was happening and beg him to keep Sir Hector away from her.

The wood came to an end and Lina saw the Castle ahead of her.

Because they could not afford gardeners except for old Ives who had been with them for forty years, the gardens were overgrown and had become a wilderness.

But the daffodils were golden in the grass under the trees and the crocuses which her mother had planted years ago were a poem of colour in several of the flower-beds which later would be full of weeds.

Lina was looking up at the Castle itself, thinking how it had stood there for centuries while the Wallinghams had played their part in the history of England.

She was still humming happily to herself as she reached the first grey wall. Then as she neared the Library window she heard voices.

Instinctively she stopped by a diamond-paved casement which was open and heard her father say:

"I had no idea you felt like this about Lina!"

"She's not told you I've proposed marriage to her?"

"No."

"Well, if you ask me, the crafty little minx is playing 'hard to get.' Whatever my reputation's been like in the past, I'll make her a good husband, and I'll settle £25,000 on her the day she marries me."

Lina drew in her breath.

Slowly her fingers had clenched until her nails dug into the soft palms.

"What's more," Sir Hector went on, "I'll pay your debts and give you a handsome allowance which'll enable you to keep up this crumbling old ruin better than it is at the moment."

There was a pause while Lina prayed that her father would tell Sir Hector he was not to be bribed, and he had no right to speak of the Castle so contemptuously.

But the Earl said nothing and after a moment Sir Hector went on:

"Come now, I'm being generous, and you know it! You lost £2,000 to Davidson last night, and I am well aware that you owe a thousand or more to Hatton. They'll be expecting payment in a month, if not sooner."

"I had a run of bad luck," the Earl remarked sourly.

"You drink too much to be a good card-player," Sir Hector answered. "Nevertheless I agree you've had a bad streak lately. But cheer up!"

He laughed before he finished:

"As my father-in-law your credit'll be quite considerable, as you're doubtless well aware!"

8

There was a sound from the Library which made Lina think that Sir Hector was rising from the chair in which he had been sitting.

"I must be going now," he said. "Tell Lina when she returns that we'll be married at the beginning of June. That'll give her time to collect her trousseau which of course, I'll pay for!"

"You seem very sure of yourself."

There was a note in the Earl's voice which told Lina that her father was at last resenting the way in which Sir Hector was behaving.

"Of course I'm sure," he replied. "What else can you do, Wallingham, but accept? You'd be a damned fool if you didn't see that it's very much to your advantage."

The last words were almost indistinct and Lina realised that Sir Hector had left the Library and was already in the passage which led to the Hall.

She waited for another few seconds before she ran past the Library window, entered the house through a garden-door and hurried up a secondary staircase which led her to her bedroom on the first floor.

She had always slept in a room in one of the towers because it had fascinated her as a child, and now when she had the whole castle to choose from, she had remained in the small but attractive room she had always loved.

It had two windows, one which looked over the garden and the woods from which she had just come and another from which there was a view of the front of the Castle and the drive with its avenue of old oaks.

She crossed the room and standing hidden by the curtains peeped towards the front door.

Outside Sir Hector was just heaving himself with some difficulty, because he was a heavy man, onto the back of a fine thoroughbred which was being held by the groom who had come with him.

He invariably brought a groom with him because, as Lina knew, the man carried the presents which he brought for her.

Now he looked to where the Earl was standing at the top of the steps under the ancient Gothic archway of the front door.

"Goodbye, Wallingham," Sir Hector said, "and don't forget to give Lina my message."

As he spoke he touched the brim of his hat with his riding-crop, then with a smile on his face which Lina thought was one of triumph, rode off.

As she watched his horse trotting down the drive she knew that she hated him with a violence that she had never felt for anybody in the whole of her life.

Then because her knees felt as if they would no longer support her she sat down on the bed and tried to think.

The smile on Sir Hector's face had been more frightening and more convincing than anything he had actually said in words.

It was a smile of victory, the smile of a man who had got exactly what he wanted and had completely annihilated any opposition there might have been to prevent it.

"I cannot marry him! I cannot!" Lina said to herself.

Then she remembered the sums of money her father owed and the allowance he had been promised.

It was perhaps that, more than anything else, that made her feel sick.

How could he stoop to being nothing more than a paid servant to a man like Sir Hector Standish?

She had always been aware that her father was in many ways a weak character, a man who found it easy to accept the good things of life from wherever they came rather than stand on his principles.

It was her mother and his love for her which had made him take his rightful place in the County, even though they were restricted by lack of money.

Now Lina was certain that the fact that they had many friends when her mother was alive was entirely due to her and not because they had any real affection for her father.

Certainly when her mother died the invitations were not so frequent, and it had therefore been easy for her father to drift into the habit of accepting the hospitality so freely offered that came from Standish Towers.

'He is making use of Papa!' Lina thought bitterly, 'and now he wishes to make use of me!'

At the same time there was a glint in Sir Hector's eyes and a note in his voice when he spoke of love which made her shrink, and ignorant though she was of the subject, she knew it was not real love he had for her, but something sinister and unpleasant.

"I hate him! I hate him!" she said violently, and rose from the bed to look at her reflection in the mirror.

Lina was not conceited, but she would have been very stupid if she was not aware that in the last year she had become very pretty.

She was, in fact, very like her mother who had been acclaimed a beauty when she had appeared in society and refused the chance of several brilliant marriages because she had fallen in love with the Earl of Wallingham.

Her parents had hesitated before giving their permission for the simple reason that the Earl was a comparatively poor man while two of their daughter's other suitors were extremely wealthy.

Finally, as they could not deny her happiness, she had been allowed to marry the Earl and to all intents and purposes they had lived happily ever after.

Their only real sadness was that after Lina was born her mother was unable to have any more children, and the Earl was therefore left without a son to inherit his title and the Castle which Sir Hector had called truthfully "a crumbling ruin."

Nevertheless it was theirs, and to Lina it was the home she loved and which she had no wish to leave unless it was for a man who could mean as much in her life as her father had meant in her mother's.

Now there was an expression of fear in her large eyes and she thought that if she was to see Sir Hector's face reflected in the mirror into which she gazed, she would wish to die.

"What can I do, Mama?" she asked aloud, turning from the dressing-table to stand in front of the portrait of her mother which hung on the wall.

It was only a crayon sketch done by an unknown artist who had been staying in the neighbourhood and who had come to the Castle to beg the Countess to sit for him because she was the most beautiful person he had ever seen.

Laughingly she had agreed and he had captured, perhaps because he had fallen in love with his subject, her beauty as a more experienced painter might not have been able to do.

The oval face with its pointed chin was almost the same as Lina's. She had the same large eyes, the small straight nose, the broad forehead, and the fair hair which seemed to have something ethereal and fairy-like about the softness of it as it haloed the exquisitely shaped head.

Because the sketch was not coloured it did not show the strangely-coloured eyes that Lina had also inherited from her mother.

They were not blue as they should have been with her particular colouring, but green flecked with gold, "like a stream in the sunshine," as the artist had said poetically.

Lina raised her eyes now to her mother's face.

"Help me...Mama," she said. "You know I cannot...marry such a...man as...Sir Hector. Save me, please...save me!"

She waited, and clearly as if her mother answered, Lina knew what she must do.

———————————————————

When Lina found herself the following morning travelling to London in a train that had left their nearest

13

railway station just after six o'clock, she could hardly believe it had been so easy to get away.

She had avoided seeing her father for the rest of the day after Sir Hector had called, but she knew he was drinking, first in the Study, then down at the local village Inn where he was always welcome amongst the village layabouts.

He had forgotten that they had a small dinner-party that evening consisting of the doctor and his wife, and their other friends, a charming couple who had recently arrived at the Manor House on the other side of the village.

Colonel Graham, who had served in the Grenadier Guards, had visited the castle a number of times and had just moved into the Manor which his wife had inherited from her father some years previously.

Lina had laid out her father's evening-clothes in his bedroom and only half-an-hour before dinner she came down to the Study to find him with a glass in his hand.

"There you are, Lina!" he said. "Where have you been? I want to talk to you."

"There is no time now, Papa," Lina had replied. "Have you forgotten the Grahams and the Emersons are coming to dinner?"

"I did not invite them."

"Yes, you did, Papa. At least you asked the Grahams, and I invited the Emersons to make us six."

She glanced at the clock and said:

"You will have to hurry as they will be here in thirty minutes. Everything is ready for you upstairs."

"I want to see Graham," the Earl said, "but I also have to talk to you, Lina."

"I am afraid it will have to wait until tomorrow morning, Papa," Lina replied.

She smiled at him and slipped from the room before he could say any more.

She had taken a great deal of trouble over dinner, helping the old Cook who was almost past her work, and making sure that the few bottles of good wine they had left in the cellar were at the right temperature.

As she expected, her father enjoyed the company of the Colonel, and the doctor, who could be very amusing and by the time they left it was easy for Lina to say goodnight and hurry away to her room without waiting to listen to anything her father had to say.

Because he had been so late the previous night and had also drunk a great deal during the day and at dinner she was sure he had forgotten what he had to tell her.

Anyway, he would be able to tell Sir Hector later quite truthfully that he had not informed her of his proposals and could not therefore be held responsible for her disappearance.

It was with the greatest difficulty that Lina had found enough ready money for the journey and to keep herself in London until she found some means of employment.

Fortunately it was the beginning of the month, and she still had a little money left that her father had given her after he had an unexpectedly good night at Standish Towers.

She had discovered in the last year that the only way she could pay for anything was to persuade her father to be generous when he had won at the tables. On this occasion he had handed her £15 of which she had half left.

She also had a few sovereigns of her own which she had secreted away against a rainy day and amongst her few possessions were a few pieces of her mother's jewellery. She was afraid they would fetch very little if she sold them and it would be agonising to part with them.

Her father had never admitted that he had sold her mother's rings and a small string of pearls she had worn, which he had always declared were in a safe place.

It had hurt Lina desperately when she realised that her mother's treasured possessions had gone to pay his gambling debts, and after that she had never reminded him that she had a sapphire ring which her mother had often worn and also a brooch set with sapphires.

"They are mine," Lina had said to herself fiercely. "I will not have them thrown away on card games which Papa well-knows he cannot afford to play!"

At the same time she was frightened because if it was a case of a debt of honour, which card games invariably were, she would, if he pleaded with her, have sold them rather than let him be disgraced.

She thought now that if she disappeared she was quite certain Sir Hector would search for her, but he would in the meantime, because he was so confident of marrying her, pay her father's debts.

"I will have to hide where he can never find me," she told herself.

This meant that it would be impossible for her to go to any of her relations because her father would obviously supply Sir Hector with their names and addresses.

As the train travelled on Lina looked unseeingly out of the window.

She tried to think out clearly and decisively what would be the best place in which she could hide.

It was obvious that she would have to earn money and she thought rather helplessly that was going to be difficult.

Her mother had insisted that she should have a good education, although that was something that was not easy living as they were in the country. Yet through sheer persistence on the Countess's part it had been achieved.

There had been teachers of all sorts on different subjects.

"I am not going to have you taught, darling," her mother had said, "by one inadequate Governess who is expected to be proficient in every subject, and is paid a pittance for her services."

Lina had learned that was what happened in most households to the girls of the family, and it was only the precious sons who were sent to Public Schools and Universities and were tutored in the holidays.

"I was lucky," the Countess had said, "and that is why I am determined, dearest, that you should be lucky too."

Her mother's luck had come about because one of her brothers was not strong enough to go to School.

He therefore had tutors at home, and as the family seat was not far from Oxford, teachers with first-class brains had been engaged. His sister had shared his lessons.

The Countess had therefore scoured the country for retired School-Masters and they either came to the Castle or Lina went to them.

On one thing her mother was very insistent, and that was that Lina should speak languages fluently.

French had been the easiest to arrange, because living not far from the Castle was the widow of an English Diplomat who was a member of a distinguished French family.

When her husband died she had felt that she was too old to return to France.

"I never liked this cold country," she had said, "but here I am, and here I must stay, although at times I find it very boring."

Lina's mother had laughed.

"I think, *Madame*," she said, "the reason why you are bored is that you have nothing much to do. So I am going to ask you to teach my daughter to speak like a Frenchwoman, and I believe you will enjoy the lessons as much as she will."

The widow had at first been astonished at such a

request, then somewhat grudgingly she agreed that she would give it a try.

The Countess's words had been prophetic. Not only did Lina enjoy her lessons, but so did her teacher, with the result that Lina became as her mother had wished, extremely proficient in French, although somewhat hesitating in Italian and German.

'Perhaps,' Lina thought now, 'my French will be useful.'

She could not think exactly how, because, if she was to be a Governess which she felt was the only career open to her, the children, if they were to be as well-educated as she was herself, would doubtless have a French teacher.

There was however no point in anticipating the worst and she forced herself to feel optimistic as before noon the train steamed into St. Pancras Station.

A porter collected Lina's luggage and when he had found her a hackney-carriage she asked the driver to take her to Mrs. Hunt's Domestic Bureau in Mount Street.

She knew it was the best Bureau in London for although at the Castle they seldom changed their servants, keeping those who were old and faithful and prepared to work for very small wages, she had heard her mother's friends recommend it.

They were always complaining about the difficulties of keeping a good staff, and the worry it was when they had to keep changing, seldom, it appeared, for the better.

"I told Mrs. Hunt myself," Lina remembered one of her mother's friends saying, "the girls she sends me nowadays are an insult, and if she sends me such creatures again I shall take my patronage elsewhere."

"I have always understood that Mrs. Hunt's is the best Bureau," the Countess said.

"Oh, it is!" the lady had agreed. "At the same time the woman is a terrible snob and she gives all the best servants to her London clients who have the highest titles and boast of being members of the Marlborough House Set."

There was a note of envy and malice in her voice which Lina did not miss.

At the same time at the back of her mind she remembered the remarks about Mrs. Hunt.

It was this that had made her write out in the early hours of the morning an excellent reference for herself.

She dated it as being written before her mother died and signed in a very good imitation of her signature.

She thought with a smile, as she itemised her excellence as a Governess and a teacher that it would be hard for a future employer to resist such a paragon.

Then when she looked at herself in the mirror she felt doubtful.

She looked very young to be in charge of children and she only hoped that Mrs. Hunt would not realise that the Countess of Wallingham's fictitious governess had been only sixteen when this letter was supposedly written.

Lina paid the cabman when they reached Mount Street and asked him to place her small trunk and carpet-bag just inside the door of the Bureau.

He obliged her, thanked her for her tip, and said:

"Good luck, Miss! If Oi was a rich man Oi'd engage yer meself!"

"Thank you," Lina replied and felt somewhat encouraged by the compliment.

She, however, felt nervous as she crossed the room, where a number of other applicants were sitting on hard benches, towards a desk at the far end.

It was occupied by an elderly woman with sharp dark eyes wearing steel spectacles, and Lina was aware she had been watching her since she entered and had not missed the fact that she had brought her luggage with her.

She was quite certain this would be interpreted as meaning she was desperate for a job of some sort and would therefore take anything she was offered.

Instinctively her chin went up a little. Although she spoke quietly and her voice was soft, she also spoke with an authority that she was not aware a real Governess in search of employment would not have used.

The woman behind the desk, who she imagined was Mrs. Hunt, did not speak. She merely looked at her in what most applicants found an intimidating manner.

"I am seeking a position as Governess," Lina said, "and I have always heard that yours is the best Domestic Bureau in the country."

She took the letter she had written last night from her handbag and placed it on the desk.

"This is my reference from the Countess of Wallingham for whom I worked for many years."

21

"You do not look old enough to have been *many* years with anybody!" Mrs. Hunt said sharply.

She picked up the letter in a manner which was meant to convey that she was not impressed.

Nevertheless, Lina noticed that she read the embossed address carefully and doubtless did not miss the coronet above it.

"What is your name?"

"Cromer—Miss Cromer."

Lina had chosen the name of one of her Governesses, a delightful woman who had taught at a fashionable school in London before she reached the age of retirement.

Mrs. Hunt finished reading the letter, then she said:

"I do not think I have anything on my books suitable at the moment, but you can sit down and wait while I look through the ledger."

"Thank you," Lina replied.

She walked a few feet to a hard bench and sat down on it facing the desk, interested to see what Mrs. Hunt would do.

She turned to her assistant, a mousy little woman who had a nervous twitch of the eyelids.

She showed her the letter, then a large ledger was lifted onto the desk in front of Mrs. Hunt, who proceeded to turn over the pages.

"What about this one?" Mrs. Hunt asked.

"Oh, no. We sent somebody there last week," the mousy woman replied.

"I'd forgotten."

Four more pages were turned and Lina began to be

worried about how long she would be able to wait for a job, coming here every day and waiting forlornly on a hard bench.

At the other end of the room there were two rosy-cheeked young girls who looked as if they had come from the country and were, she was sure, seeking employment as scullery maids in some nobleman's house.

There was a middle-aged woman in a beaded bonnet who she thought might be a Housekeeper, or perhaps a Head Housemaid, and a stocky young man who from his gaiters and the cap he was twisting in his hands must be looking for a position as a groom.

Lina longed to ask them how many days they had been waiting, but knew it was something she should not do.

Then she heard Mrs. Hunt say in a voice which she was not supposed to overhear:

"What about Lady Birchington? I thought she was wanting somebody."

"Not a Governess," the mousy woman replied. "She wants a lady's maid and she has to speak French."

Mrs. Hunt snorted.

"We're not likely to find that in a hurry!"

Without really thinking, Lina rose and walked to the desk.

"I speak French fluently," she declared.

Mrs. Hunt stared at her.

"The client I was discussing with my colleague," she said in a tone that was meant to rebuke Lina for listening, "requires a lady's-maid, not a Governess."

23

"I am quite prepared to take it if that is all you have available," Lina said.

Mrs. Hunt raised her eye-brows.

"I should have thought that such a subservient position would be beneath you."

"I need a post immediately," Lina replied, "and I am therefore not prepared to be too particular."

She thought as she spoke that the position of lady's-maid would be an even more effective place of concealment.

She was quite certain Sir Hector would not think to look for her in somebody's Servants' Hall.

Mrs. Hunt bent towards the mousy woman and whispered in her ear.

The mousy woman whispered back and it seemed to Lina that they both metaphorically shrugged their shoulders.

"Very well," Mrs. Hunt said. "You can contact Her Ladyship and say we've sent you. I'll give you the card of introduction and at least Her Ladyship can't say that we've not done our best to oblige her."

There was no doubt that Mrs. Hunt felt she had little chance of getting the job.

However, Lina told herself optimistically, it would be interesting to see what happened.

Aloud she said:

"Thank you very much, and would you be kind enough to keep my name on your books just in case I am unsuccessful, in which case I will be back."

Mrs. Hunt did not deign to reply to this.

She merely wrote out a card, her assistant placed

it in an envelope and handed it over the top of the desk to Lina with her reference.

Lina took both envelopes.

"Thank you very much. You have been very kind."

It was obvious that Mrs. Hunt was surprised by her gratitude, but she did not speak and Lina walked away towards the door conscious that the other occupants of the room were staring at her in a somewhat hostile fashion because she had been successful.

As she reached her luggage she picked up the carpetbag but looked a little helplessly at her trunk.

Then she glanced at the young man who looked like a groom and who was watching her.

It took him a second or two to understand what she wanted, then he got to his feet.

"Oi'll give ye a 'and, Miss."

"Thank you very much," Lina replied.

They went outside and after waiting only a minute or two, a cab with a tired horse came driving down the street.

It stopped and the young man lifted the trunk up onto the box beside the cabman.

Lina put her carpet-bag inside. Then she debated whether or not to offer the young man a tip, but remembered that she herself was now a servant.

"Thank you," she said, and held out her hand.

"Pleasure, Oi'm sure. Pleased ter meet yer," he said, "an' Oi wishes yer luck."

"I wish you the same," Lina replied.

As she drove off to the address which Mrs. Hunt had given her she thought that while she seemed to

25

be successful with the lower classes which she had now joined, it remained to be seen how she would fare with those she must now look up to as her betters.

Chapter Two

ANY MAN entering the Drawing-Room of 23 Belgrave Square would have stared open-mouthed at the three Ladies seated round the fire.

They were all of them famous for their beauty, and even in an age when there were many beautiful women in London, these particular three were outstanding.

The Prince of Wales, who was an acknowledged expert on female beauty, had said he could not have imagined any woman could be so sensationally beautiful as the Marchioness of Holme.

But the Countess of Pendock ran her very close with hair that was as golden as the sun and eyes as blue as the sea, while Lady Birchington had not only outstanding beauty, but a fascination which most men found irresistible.

Kitty Birchington was at the moment wearing an extremely becoming new tea-gown which had been especially designed for her by Lucille.

When she had entered the Drawing-Room her two friends had exclaimed both in admiration and in envy at her appearance and she had therefore arranged herself rather self-consciously on a satin sofa.

It was not only a perfect background for her white skin and her red hair, but also for her pale green tea-gown. It had an exquisite trimming of silver lace and tiny pearl buttons which would intrigue and bemuse any man who attempted to undo them.

As soon as they seated themselves Kitty Birchington had exclaimed:

"I have so much to tell you! That is why I sent notes to you both immediately after breakfast to tell you to meet me here at five."

"What has happened?" Daisy Holme enquired.

As she spoke the large diamond ear-rings which glittered in her small ears and the ostrich feathers which fluttered in her hat seemed to accentuate the darkness of her hair and the winged brows over the velvet depths of her eyes.

Kitty Birchington clasped her hands together.

"Hold your breath," she said, "for you will never believe what I have to say!"

"You are in love again?" Evie Pendock hazarded.

Kitty laughed.

"I am in love, but that is not what I have to tell you."

"Then what is it?"

Kitty drew in her breath before she replied:

"Fabian has finished with Alice!"

For a moment her two friends stared at her in astonishment.

Then Daisy exclaimed:

"I do not believe you! It is impossible! Fabian's affairs always last longer than that!"

"I agree with you," Evie said. "They have not been together for more than a few months, and Fabian always boasts that his affairs last as long as his heart beats! Besides Alice is very lovely!"

There was a sarcastic note which belied the compliment, then both Daisy and Evie looked at Kitty waiting for an explanation.

"Alice came to see me yesterday evening," she began only to be interrupted with the cry:

"Alice is back in London? I had no idea! Why did nobody tell us?"

"Because she has no wish to see anybody but me," Kitty answered. "She is devastated! Broken-hearted! But then Alice was always slightly hysterical!"

The two friends obviously agreed with what she said and she continued:

"She cannot understand why she has lost Fabian. She said he had grown restless, made excuses not to make love to her, and finally admitted that he was bored."

There was silence. Then Daisy said sharply:

"Well, all I can say is she must have been extremely stupid! When I saw them together two months ago Fabian was paying her attention in his usual devastating manner, and seemed delighted to squire her everywhere."

"That is the way Fabian always behaves," Evie said, "but that it should actually be over so quickly is astounding!"

"That was what I thought," Kitty agreed, "and as we ourselves were all so very much more successful with Fabian, I knew you would be interested."

"I am very curious to know what happened," Daisy said ruminatively.

Again there was silence until Evie said:

"If you ask me, Alice is really rather a bore."

"I agree with you," Daisy replied. "At the same time, Fabian never exactly talks to the woman with whom he is in love."

"What you are saying, Daisy, is that there is no time," Kitty said. "When one is with Fabian, all one wants are his kisses and a great deal more, and what is so infuriating, if we are honest, is that Fabian is always the one who stops loving first."

She paused before she added slowly:

"It is rather horrid of me, but because I have always thought Alice besides being boring is rather a cold woman, I hoped she might, although of course it would have been a miracle, teach Fabian a lesson."

"Do you mean?" Evie asked, "that he might have been more in love with her than she was with him?"

"Exactly!" Kitty agreed.

She sighed.

"I suppose there is not a woman born who would not love Fabian crazily and uncontrollably and feel her heart was broken when he left her."

"As we all know," Daisy murmured.

She stared into the fire as she went on:

"I do not think I have ever been so unhappy as when Fabian said goodbye but I hope I had enough dignity and self-respect not to whine about it, or let anybody be aware how much I minded. In fact you are the only two people to whom I have ever spoken about him."

"You know we can sympathise and understand as nobody else could," Kitty said. "I have always rather resented the fact that I could not hold him for more than two years."

"Eighteen months!" Evie corrected in a low voice, but Kitty ignored her.

"At the same time," Daisy said, "whatever I suffered, I shall always be grateful in a way to Fabian because he taught me so much about love. I suppose Frenchmen are born with a knowledge that Englishmen never learn."

"Of course they are," Kitty agreed. "Frenchmen start thinking about women when they are in the cradle, and they have their first love-affairs while Englishmen are counting how many runs they have made at cricket or totting up the pheasants they have brought down since they first started to shoot."

Evie laughed and added:

"While, of course, a Frenchman is counting the hearts he has broken!"

"Exactly!" Daisy agreed. "Without being spiteful, I wish just for once, that Fabian's heart would at least crack, and he could feel some of the pangs of loss that we have all experienced."

Kitty sighed.

"It is a waste of time wishing," she said. "He is the most attractive man in Europe, and there is not a woman born who is able to resist him."

"I am sure you are right," Daisy agreed, "and in the Society in which Fabian moves in France and England he is not likely to encounter much resistance, let alone anything so astonishing as a rebuff."

"No, of course not," Kitty agreed, "and perhaps it is very shaming to admit it, but if Fabian so much as lifted his little finger we all three of us would go running back to him like hypnotised rabbits!"

"I am sure I would do nothing of the sort!" Daisy exclaimed.

"Of course you would!" Kitty insisted. "Who could resist any man who looks like Fabian, talks like Fabian and makes love like Fabian?"

There was silence after she had spoken while all three women looked reminiscently into the fire, their eyes soft with memories of a man who, as Daisy had said, had taught them about love and made them find it a very different emotion from what they had ever known before.

In the Marlborough House Set to which they belonged it was accepted that after a Lady had been married for five to ten years and had presented her husband with a son and heir and perhaps two other children, she was entitled to a love-affair if it was discreet.

The Prince of Wales had set the pace by being infatuated with many beautiful women, but still showing to the public an image of a happily married man with his lovely wife, Alexandra.

He had passed through some tempestuous *affaires de coeur* with Lily Langtry, with the alluring Lady Brooke with whom he had been wildly infatuated, and now, as every hostess knew, he could not enjoy a party unless the fascinating Mrs. Keppel was at his side.

Daisy Holme had enjoyed a fiery affair with one of her husband's best friends before Fabian, the *Duc* de Saverne, had come into her life.

She had met him when he was still enamoured with Evie Pendock and to all intents and purposes had taken him from her.

But Evie knew that he had, in fact, already been growing a little restless, and because the transports of delight they had enjoyed together were dying down it was inevitable what would happen when Daisy came on the scene.

The *Duc's* affair with Daisy had been facilitated by the fact that the Marquess was such a keen sportsman that he left his wife alone for long periods when he was either shooting or fishing in other parts of the British Isles.

Lord Birchington on the other hand, attended every race-meeting whether or not he had one of his horses running, and Kitty's affair with the *Duc* only came to an end when, during the winter, there was no racing, and it became difficult for them to spend much time with each other.

The three husbands in question must have been vaguely aware of what was taking place, but because it was expected they should close their eyes to anything but a flagrant breach of decorum they said nothing.

But there were rumours that the *Duc* de Saverne's attentions to pretty women were not always accepted so philosophically.

Duels in France happened frequently where he was

concerned and he had been challenged, somebody had once said jokingly, by outraged husbands from every country in Europe!

Kitty had often thought that perhaps if George had made a fuss about her liaison with the *Duc* it would have brought a spice of danger to the love-affair which had been lacking.

But George either intentionally or unintentionally had been more subtle. He had merely returned home when there was no racing and entertained the *Duc* himself, instead of disappearing to his Club as was expected of him.

'Fabian was bored not with me, but with George!' Kitty thought now, and it was an idea with which she was able to console herself.

At the same time she knew that it was not entirely true and Fabian had inevitably gone in search of pastures new, or more explicitly a new woman to whom he could make love in his fascinating, irresistible manner.

"I think we have to face the fact," Daisy said, "that as long as Fabian is alive he will walk the primrose path, basking in the sunshine, while women fall into his arms like fragrant flowers which fade all too quickly, and he throws them away to pick yet another."

Evie and Kitty both laughed.

"Oh, Daisy, you are quite poetical," Kitty said, "but I for one hope that Fabian on his 'primrose path' will be caught in a hailstorm, and now I am really being spiteful!"

"There is not the slightest chance of it," Daisy replied.

"Why are you so positive?" Evie asked.

"I will tell you why," Daisy answered. "Because Fabian chooses his loves from what the newspapers call 'The upper classes.'"

"What has that got to do with it?"

"My father said once, and I am sure it is true, that the upper classes are always open to temptation, while the lower classes take to loving because it is a cheap entertainment, and it is only the middle-classes who are respectable!"

Everybody laughed.

"I am sure your father was right," Kitty said, "though I have never heard it put quite like that, and of course it is well-known that the middle-classes in England are strictly moral."

"So are the *bourgeoisie* in France," Evie added.

"I think we all agree that Fabian looks through Debrett and the Almanack de Gotha before he starts his very well rehearsed act of seduction," Kitty smiled.

"No, Fabian prides himself," Daisy contradicted, "that he can tell at a glance not only a woman's antecedents, but also her character."

"Did he really say that to you?" Kitty asked with interest. "He always told me how fastidious he was, which I suppose amounts to the same thing."

"All Frenchmen are snobs," Daisy replied. "I heard it said of Fabian once and I remember how much it annoyed me, that there was not a Duchess on either side of the Channel under thirty-five who had not entertained him in her bed!"

"That is an exaggeration," Evie remarked, "but undoubtedly it has a grain of truth in it. If you think about it, Fabian's lady-loves have always been like ourselves, and of course Alice is the daughter of a Duke."

"That obviously did not help her to keep him!" Kitty said.

"I was just thinking," Evie remarked, "of the other women we know with whom Fabian has amused himself, and I must admit the theory that he insists on their being what is vulgarly called '*la crème de la crème*' is true."

"Well, we shall soon see who is his new partner at the Ball on Saturday," Daisy said, "and I have a feeling because he has finished with Alice that it will be a Frenchwoman."

"Shall we have a bet on it?" Evie asked.

"I would not waste my money," Kitty said, "and quite frankly, I do not care who Fabian makes love to, as long as I do not have to have them crying on my shoulder when he says goodbye."

"It sounds as if you had a difficult time with Alice," Daisy remarked.

"You know what Alice is like," Kitty answered. "She wept and went on saying over and over again that she could not think how it happened and how much she loved him."

"She certainly behaved rather indiscreetly," Evie said. "Everybody knew they went to the South of France together, and I was told they were behaving outrageously at Monte Carlo. But then Alice has never shown very much sense."

"It was the first time she had ever been in love,"

Daisy recalled. "As you said, Kitty, I think she is a cold woman and when the temperature turns the other way that sort always behaves outrageously."

Evie sat up straight in her chair.

"I believe you have just given us the explanation of why Fabian was bored so quickly."

"What is that?" Daisy asked.

"That Fabian enjoys igniting a fire, but when there is nothing he can add to it, he lets it burn itself out."

Both Daisy and Kitty stared at her, then as they were about to reply the Butler came into the room.

There was silence as he walked to his mistress and handed her a card on a silver salver.

Lady Birchington picked it up and said:

"I had forgotten you told me this woman was calling again. Put her in the Morning-Room."

"Very good, M'Lady."

He had turned and was walking towards the door when Kitty asked:

"Is there any point in my seeing her? What is she like, Bateson?"

Bateson hesitated for a moment before he replied:

"She is, M'Lady, a very lovely young lady."

Kitty looked at him in astonishment.

"*Lady*, Bateson?"

"Yes, M'Lady!"

She looked down at the card she held in her hand.

"I do not understand."

The Butler said nothing and after a moment Daisy remarked:

"What is worrying you?"

"I am just surprised at what Bateson said," Kitty answered. "I asked Mrs. Hunt for a lady's-maid who could speak French. I am not going to stay in Paris with an English maid who cannot communicate with the rest of the staff, or do any shopping for me, but the Bureau is making a terrible fuss about finding one."

She looked down again at the card before she said:

"This woman has been with the late Countess of Wallingham. I have never heard of her."

"I know the name," Daisy said. "And I think I have heard my father speak of the Earl, but I am sure I have never met them."

"If you want somebody who can speak French," Evie said, "you had better see this woman, Kitty, and snap her up while you can. I shall have to take my maid with me, who cannot speak a word of the language and would not try even if I paid her to do so, but I certainly could not trust my clothes to anybody else."

"Your maid Jones is indispensable," Daisy said, "and that is what I feel about my old horror, who has been with me for ten years, unlike Kitty, who has been unlucky with her lady's-maids."

"The one I have just lost was not too bad," Kitty remarked, "but she said her mother was dying. So here I am going to the smartest Ball in Paris without anybody even to unpack my trunk!"

"I should go to see what this woman is like," Daisy suggested.

"I will but I am actually in no hurry. I am not dining until late."

"Go now," Evie said, "so that we can carry on with our fascinating conversation about Fabian."

"What a bore servants are," Kitty complained.

But she rose from the sofa as she spoke and moved slowly and gracefully towards the door which the Butler was holding open for her.

As she disappeared Daisy said:

"It is strange that Bateson should describe the woman as a 'young *Lady*.' I have known him for years as he was a footman with us before he came to Kitty, and I have never known him to make a mistake in judging the status of a caller."

Evie smiled.

"Yes, Bateson is quite a character, and I think however unfortunate Kitty may be with her other servants she is lucky to have him."

Bateson was at that moment opening the door of the Morning-Room into which he had shown Lina.

She had called at Belgrave Square after leaving Mrs. Hunt's Bureau only to learn that Lady Birchington was out to luncheon, and could not be seen until five o'clock.

She wondered helplessly how she could fill in the hours and what she could do about her luggage. The only person she could consult was the cab-driver, and he was surprisingly helpful.

He drove her to Victoria Station which was not far away, told her to leave her baggage in the 'Left Luggage Office,' then sit in the "Ladies Waiting Room" until it was time for her to return to Belgrave Square.

"Yer'll be safe there, Miss," he said, "an' if yer

39

takes my advice yer won't go wandering about on yer own. The streets ain't safe for someun as young an' pretty as yerself."

Lina thanked him profusely, but when she tried to give him an extra large tip for being so helpful he had refused it.

"Oi'll tak what's right, an' no more," he said. "Keep yer money safe, 'cos you'll be wantin' it for yerself if yer don't get the job yer after."

"If they should refuse to take me, can you recommend anywhere where I could stay?" Lina enquired.

After careful consideration the cabman wrote down an address of what he said was a respectable lodging and where she would "come to no harm."

Lina was not quite certain what he meant by that, but she supposed there were places where she might be robbed of her money and her clothes. The idea was very frightening.

She had therefore done exactly as she had been told and sat rather forlornly in the Waiting Room listening to the trains come and go until a quarter to five.

Then she had taken another cab to carry her back to Belgrave Square.

She had been impressed not so much by the size of the house as by the elegance with which it was furnished.

There were huge vases of malmaison carnations in the Hall and in the Morning-Room into which she had been shown which scented the air with their fragrance.

When Lady Birchington came into the room in her green tea-gown, Lina thought admiringly that nobody could be more beautiful or more alluring.

She watched her and only when she reached her side did Lina remember she should curtsy.

If Lina was surprised by Kitty Birchington's looks, one glance at the girl waiting for her made Kitty raise her eye-brows.

Bateson was right. She was not only lovely, but she certainly looked a Lady.

"Who are you?" she asked sharply, feeling that perhaps somebody was playing a joke on her.

"My name is Cromer."

"I know that!" Kitty answered. "I have read the card you brought with you, but you do not look to me like a lady's-maid."

"I was hoping for a post as Governess," Lina replied, "but Mrs. Hunt told me that you need somebody who speaks French, and it is a language in which I am very fluent."

"Why? Have you lived in France?"

"No, My Lady, but I was taught by a Frenchwoman and I find no difficulty in reading, writing, and speaking the language."

"But you have never been a lady's-maid before?"

As she spoke Kitty seated herself in an armchair, but she did not invite Lina to sit down, so she remained standing.

"I looked after the Countess of Wallingham's clothes when she was short-handed."

"I think really you are too young for the position," Kitty said slowly, "and too..."

She stopped. She was about to say "too pretty" then thought that would be a mistake.

She saw the expression of disappointment in Lina's

face. There was a little pause before Lina said:

"Oh, please . . . give me a chance. I learn very quickly, and I know I shall be able to do exactly what you . . . require of me. I am sure I will get on well with the rest of your staff . . . and I promise that I am very . . . adaptable."

Kitty stared at her. Then suddenly she said:

"You talk in a very educated way."

"I have been well-educated," Lina replied, then added a little late: "My Lady."

"So that is why you thought you would be a Governess."

"I am certain, My Lady, I could teach children of almost any age."

Kitty did not answer. She just stared at Lina.

Suddenly she rose to her feet.

"Stay here!" she said. "I will come back in a few minutes."

She walked quickly from the room leaving Lina staring after her in surprise.

She wondered what she had said that perhaps had been wrong. At the same time she was not yet dismissed.

"Please God, let her take me," she prayed. "I am sure Sir Hector would never find me here . . . and I have never heard Papa speak of the Birchingtons."

Because there was no point in standing when she was alone, Lina sat down in a chair and went on praying.

"Do you really think she is capable of playing such a part?" Daisy enquired. "She sounds like a school-girl."

"She is lovely! Really lovely," Kitty replied, "by any standards, even ours."

She looked at the incredulous expression on her friend's face and added:

"See her for yourself."

"Now wait a minute," Daisy said. "Sit down and let us think this out. What you are suggesting is that we should play a trick on Fabian."

"We will teach him a lesson he will never forget," Kitty interposed.

Daisy laughed.

"Are you really suggesting, Kitty, you should take this young woman to Paris and pretend she is somebody important? And do you really think Fabian will fall in love with her? Why should he?"

"It is a gamble," Kitty admitted.

"Of course it is, and for all we know he may have somebody else already, in which case if he is in the middle of a love-affair he would not be interested in the Venus di Milo!"

"From what Alice said to me, I do not believe there is anybody else."

"Well, we will have to act quickly," Evie said, "or it will be too late."

"That is true," Daisy replied. "After all, today is Saturday and we are off to Paris next Thursday."

There was silence before Evie asked:

"How do you know she is middle-class and respectable?"

"Well, for one thing, she really wanted to be a Governess," Kitty replied, "and I suppose that Governesses are middle-class. Anyway, let us have her in and ask her. We have nothing to lose by it."

"No, of course not," Daisy agreed, "and I am certainly keen to see this creature who Bateson refers to as a 'lovely young Lady,' and who you think will constitute a bait for Fabian."

"If you ask me, the whole thing is too far-fetched," Evie said. "At the same time I am quite prepared to say that it would be extremely amusing for us if Fabian is deceived into making a fool of himself over somebody who is not what he thinks her to be."

"That is the whole point," Kitty said. "He fancies himself as such a good judge of character, and since he is quite certain he can distinguish the real from the false, the gold from the dross, it would infuriate him to be proved wrong."

"Kitty's right, you know," Evie said. "I remember Fabian once said to me: 'No woman can deceive me. I know if they are lying as soon as they open their lips.'"

"Well, I believe we can deceive him," Kitty said. "Shall I send for this woman?"

"You must not be offended," Daisy said, "if I tell you when I have seen her that I think you are making a mistake. After all, we will have to dress her, pay to take her to Paris, and she will either have to stay with you, or with one of us."

"She will stay with me," Kitty said. "It is my idea, and I intend to coach her so that she makes no mistakes if Fabian is interested in her."

"And if he is not?"

Kitty laughed.

"Then she can go back to Mrs. Hunt and look for another job!"

"Which will doubtless be very much easier than the one we are offering her!"

All three laughed and Kitty reached out her hand to pull the bell.

Bateson answered it almost immediately which suggested that he had been waiting outside in the Hall sensing that something was going on.

"Ask Miss Cromer to come in here," Kitty said.

"Very good, M'Lady."

It seemed as if the three friends had nothing to say to each other before Bateson reappeared.

"Miss Cromer, M'Lady!" he announced and Lina came into the room.

She was thinking as she moved towards the little group by the fireplace that the Drawing-Room was even more beautiful than the Morning-Room, and the aroma of malmaison carnations which stood in vases on every table was almost overpowering.

Then when she reached the three ladies she felt they were staring at her in a critical manner which made her lift her chin a little.

At the same time she appreciated how beautiful they were and wished her mother could see them.

She thought she recognised the Marchioness of

45

Holme, having seen her pictures in the *"Ladies Journel,"* only she was much more beautiful than in print.

Kitty Birchington spoke.

"These are my friends, Miss Cromer, and we would like you to tell us something about yourself."

Lina had been expecting this and she replied:

"What do you wish to know, My Lady?"

"Who is your father? What does he do?"

"He...owns some acres of land in Huntingdonshire."

"Then he is a farmer," Kitty said.

Lina did not contradict her.

She was anxious to tell as few lies as possible and her father had, in fact, farmed at one time. But he found it was too expensive and instead had let the land out to tenants who paid unfortunately, very low rents.

"And your mother is alive?"

"No, My Lady, she is...dead."

"Do you have any brothers or sisters?"

"No, My Lady."

Kitty looked at Evie and Daisy as if for support and Daisy said:

"Would you describe yourself as middle-class, Miss Cromer?"

Lina was surprised at the question. Then she thought that as a Governess that was what she would be expected to be and she replied:

"I think that is...an accurate description."

"And you consider yourself respectable? In other words, you are a good girl."

Lina looked at her in a puzzled way.

"What my friend is asking," Evie interposed, "is

whether you indulge in love-affairs of any sort."

"N–no...of course...not!" Lina replied positively.

She had an idea they were referring to the way some of the younger servants met men in the Park and sat with their arms around each other under the trees, until her mother had heard about it.

She supposed it was the sort of way Lady Birchington would not wish her to behave if she applied for the job as lady's-maid.

But even to think of love made her remember Sir Hector, and before she could be asked any more questions she added almost angrily:

"I can assure you, My Lady, I have been very strictly and properly brought up, and it is not the sort of thing I would do anyway!"

She saw Lady Birchington smile at her friends.

"I was sure that you would feel like that," Kitty said, "and I would like you to assure me that if you were tempted into any indiscretion, or if any man should ask you to behave in a manner which your father and mother would consider improper you would refuse him."

Lina thought she should be insulted by these questions, but she supposed they might be the sort of things a Lady would ask of somebody she intended to employ.

"I can assure Your Ladyship," she replied, "that I am not interested in men, but only in finding employment and doing what is required to the very best of my ability."

Again she thought from the expression on Lady

Birchington's face that she had said the right thing.

Then Kitty said:

"I have a proposition to put to you, Miss Cromer, and I think it would be best if you sat down and listened to what I have to say."

Lina looked around and saw a chair near the sofa on which Lady Birchington was seated. She sat down on the edge of it, thinking it would be a mistake to look too comfortable.

For a moment Lady Birchington seemed at a loss for words. Then she said:

"Have you acted a part in a play?"

"Only in Charades at Christmas," Lina replied.

She was thinking as she spoke of the parties which her mother gave at the Castle and how all the children had congregated there with their parents.

She had also been asked to parties at which over the years the entertainment had varied from playing "Oranges and Lemons" and "Musical Chairs" to dancing reels and acting Charades.

"I would like you to play a part," Kitty said.

"What sort of part?" Lina enquired.

"Let us not go into it now," Kitty replied looking at Daisy as if for collaboration.

"Of course, you may want to refuse," Daisy said, "but I think, Kitty, we must make it clear to Miss Cromer that if she plays this part skillfully she will be rewarded for her efforts."

"Yes, of course," Kitty agreed.

She realised that Daisy was warning her that as she appeared so respectable Lina might refuse point-blank to entertain their suggestion of pretending to be what she was not.

It was something they had not discussed and Kitty realised now she had been rather obtuse in not thinking that a reward was necessary.

"What I suggest, Miss Cromer, is that if you do what we ask of you and play the role successfully, I will give you £100 when we return to England."

Lina looked astonished.

£100 seemed to her to be a lot of money and certainly very much more than she could earn as a Governess or a lady's-maid.

Then it struck her that these ladies might wish her to do something reprehensible and she said quickly:

"Before I accept your proposition, My Lady, I would like first to hear what it is you want me to do."

"Yes, of course," Kitty agreed.

She drew in her breath before she said:

"I want you to come with me to Paris and play the part of an English Lady of Quality. It should not be too difficult for you to do so, considering you have told me that you have been well-educated."

"I...I am afraid I do not...understand," Lina said. "Why should I be expected to play...this part?"

She thought if they wanted her to act on the stage it was something she must refuse immediately.

Her mother always told her that actresses were a race apart, and the stories of the young men who took actresses out in London and spent a fortune on them were often discussed by her mother's visitors.

They were horrified by such behaviour especially

49

when the young "men about town" who were wasting their money in such a wild manner were their sons.

"It will not be a part on the stage," Kitty said quickly. "You will pretend to be my friend and to belong to the Social World to which I belong. We are all going to a Ball next Saturday night given by the *Duc* de Saverne in Paris. I want you to make yourself pleasant to him as any Lady would do, and I hope that he will find you attractive."

Lina's eyes widened until they seemed to fill her whole face.

"I still do not...understand," she said. "Why should you...want me to do...this?"

"That is our business!" Kitty said sharply. "There is no point in your knowing more than I have told you. I should have thought any woman in your position would have jumped at the chance of a visit to Paris, if nothing else."

"But...of course I would love to go to Paris," Lina said, "but I cannot understand exactly what you wish...me to do, and I am frightened that I shall...fail you."

"I have a feeling," Kitty said, "that you will be very competent."

She looked at her two friends as if for confirmation, and saw that they agreed with her.

Lina had no idea that because she looked so lovely and sounded so sincere, all three ladies were thinking that any man, and especially the *Duc*, would find her irresistible.

"That is settled then," Kitty said with a note of triumph in her voice.

"I feel perhaps Miss Cromer is not quite convinced," Daisy said, "and I therefore have a suggestion to make."

"What is that?" Kitty asked.

"If you are giving Miss Cromer £100 on completion of our visit, then I will give her another £50 to be paid before she goes and I am sure Evie will do the same. That means she will have £200 in payment for what I feel she will not find a very arduous task."

"£200?" Lina murmured beneath her breath.

She could hardly believe it!

She knew that this would ensure there would be no need for her to return to the Castle for such a long time that she was certain that Sir Hector would give up all hope of finding her.

It was of course a very strange proposition and she was still a little nervous of exactly what it entailed.

Then she told herself with a sudden lift of her heart that to go to a Ball would be exactly what her mother would have wished for her.

She was sure that the Ball which was being attended by Lady Birchington and her friends would be one of those that were written up in the Court Column of the newspapers as being one of the most important engagements of the Season.

"Thank you very much," she said aloud looking at Kitty. "I am very pleased to accept your offer and I promise I shall do my very, very best to please you."

"That is what we want you to say," Kitty replied, "and now we have four days in which to find you the right clothes and to instruct you in what exactly you are to do."

She looked at Daisy and Evie as she said:

"I shall need your help, especially where clothes are concerned. You are well aware it would be impossible to have anything made up in four days."

"Yes, of course," Evie agreed. "As Miss Cromer is about my size, I imagine I have quite a number of gowns that would fit her with a little alteration."

"We had better give her one sensational gown to wear at the Ball," Daisy said. "As a matter of fact I have ordered one which is half-finished, and I will sacrifice that and start again. I think you will admit, Kitty, that my contribution is quite a considerable one."

"Thank you Daisy," Kitty said. "I know that the heroine's appearance in Act I is very important, but I am wondering what will happen in Act III."

"That is what I was thinking," Daisy replied.

Then she laughed.

"Oh, Kitty, you have thought of some mad schemes in your time, but I swear this is the maddest, though at the same time the most intriguing! But then I have always thought you had an agile and sharp little brain!"

"You may compliment me later," Kitty said complacently. "For the moment all we have to think of is Fabian and remember how much we all 'owe' him in one way or another!"

"Yes, of course," Daisy laughed, "and that is exactly the right word, Kitty. We 'owe' him a very special surprise, which is exactly what he is going to get!"

Chapter Three

IN THE train for Paris Lina felt as if she was moving in a dream.

She could hardly believe that what she had been experiencing these last five days was anything but a figment of her imagination.

Then she told herself it was stupid to be afraid and apprehensive of what might happen.

With the money she had herself and the £100 which she had carefully put in a Bank in London she was independent.

If she was unhappy or was asked to do anything which her mother would think wrong, she could always come home and return at least half of the money which had been paid her until she could find another job and free herself of debt towards Lady Birchington and her friends.

She had learned since she had been living in Belgrave Square that Lady Birchington was a very determined woman.

She also had a fiery temper and invariably had her own way.

The servants were frightened of her and Lina, although she assured herself there was no need to be, was frightened also.

But actually everything that was happening was so intriguing, so unexpected, that she felt she was acting a part not on the stage but in a dream that had no reality about it.

She could hardly believe it was possible that she was to own the gowns that Lady Birchington gave her. When she was given the first three, she had said:

"They are lovely, and I will be very careful for I would not wish to damage them before I return them to you."

"They are yours!" Kitty said sharply. "I assure you I shall have no further use for them."

Lina understood that behind her generosity was a note of revulsion against being expected to wear anything worn by somebody else, while she in her position was, of course, not allowed to be particular.

She smiled, and at the same time thought she should not be proud, for she would have been foolish not to be extremely grateful to receive gowns that not only had cost large sums of money, but made her look beautiful and fashionable.

When she tried them on and looked in the mirror she realised she was transformed.

Never had she expected to own silk petticoats, silk stockings, and be dressed in a way that made her feel that she was a complete stranger.

It was ridiculous to think that clothes did not matter.

Lina could not help knowing that having been a pretty but dowdy young woman, she now looked, when dressed in one of Lady Birchington's gowns not the least like her old self, but rather a Princess out of a fairy-tale.

She still could not quite understand what she was expected to do, or why she was being dressed up to appear in some strange charade that concerned all three of the beautiful ladies who were journeying to Paris for a very special Ball.

The jokes that they made between themselves, the remarks Lina could not understand, and the inescapable feeling that they were up to some mischief all made her apprehensive.

At the same time she thought she would be very stupid if she did not accept the gift that the gods had given her, which was a journey to Paris.

"I wish I could take you to Paris, dearest," her mother had said more than once. "Your father and I went there on our honeymoon, and it is not only a very romantic city but a very beautiful one, and to me a City of Love."

She looked so lovely as she spoke that Lina hoped that one day she would have memories which would bring such an expression to her eyes and smile to her lips.

It had always seemed to her, that even when she saw the name Paris printed on the Atlas it had a light surrounding it.

So she could not imagine anything more exciting

than to meet the French people and know without being conceited that she could speak their language fluently.

'I am very grateful!' she thought every night when she went to bed in the small, but attractive room she had been allotted in Lady Birchington's house in Belgrave Square.

Apart from the Luxury, the comfort and the delicious food, she was safe from Sir Hector, knowing that he, at any rate, would never be able to enter the world in which Lady Birchington and her friends shone like stars.

"Thank You...thank You...God," she said in her prayers over and over again and was already aware of how fortunate she was.

"Now we will start as we mean to go on," Lady Birchington said the first evening in the tone of a School-Mistress. "I will send somebody to fetch your luggage, although I expect there is nothing there that will be of the slightest use to you. You will stay here as my friend, Lady Littleton."

Kitty and her friends had decided that should be Lina's name after some discussion in which she took no part.

They had turned over the pages of Debrett until Daisy had said:

"I am sure we are wasting our time. Fabian thinks his instinct is superior to any reference book, and I am quite certain he will accept Lina's title without question."

They kept her Christian name because, as Kitty said, rather grudgingly, it was quite attractive.

"What about Bateson?" Evie had asked.

"There is no need to worry about him," Kitty replied. "Bateson is the soul of discretion and if I tell him Lina's name was Littleton when she came here he will forget that she ever had another one."

"I think Littleton sounds quite plausible," Daisy said, "and where is her husband supposed to be?"

"Fishing in Scotland," Kitty replied. "Interested only in what he catches. Men are all alike!"

"It would be better for him to be much older than Lina," Evie suggested, "and not particularly interested in her. I am sure it will make Fabian fancy his chances as a Knight Errant."

"A role at which he is an expert!" Daisy said sarcastically.

At the same time it was a slight variation on the original theme, and they all laughed again. But Lina listening had no idea what they were talking about.

She wondered vaguely who Fabian was, but for the next few days she found it difficult to think of anything but her clothes and the instructions which Kitty gave her.

These concerned her behaviour and the people she was going to meet, and it all became so bewildering that she sometimes felt as if she was Alice in Wonderland at the Mad-Hatter's Tea-Party.

She found it surprisingly tiring to try on clothes and stand for hours while they were altered.

So she did not think it strange, nor did she feel neglected when she was either left at home when Kitty Birchington was visiting friends, or sent to bed after dinner while her hostess went to a party to which she had of course not been invited.

'At least I shall go to one Ball in Paris,' she thought and knew it would be the most exciting thing that had ever happened in her life.

The gown the Marchioness had given her was so beautiful that she could hardly believe she was to wear it, and knew exactly how Cinderella must have felt when she was dressed by the wave of her Fairy Godmother's wand.

Kitty had taken her to Lucille's and explained that as she had arrived unexpectedly in London and was going with them to Paris, the Marchioness had sacrificed her gown that was half-finished so that Lina could have it.

White and silver, embroidered with diamanté, it was so lovely that from the moment she first saw it, Lina was certain again she had walked into a dream.

"How can you possibly give me anything so wonderful?" she had asked the Marchioness who had merely smiled and said enigmatically:

"I am prepared to make a sacrifice in a good cause."

Lina had no idea what the "good cause" could be, although she supposed it was something to do with the man they talked of incessantly who was called 'Fabian.'

It was only the day before they actually left for France that she understood that Fabian was actually giving the Ball they were all attending on Saturday night.

It was then she began to wonder why he concerned

these three ladies so greatly, and while they talked about him their conversation always seemed to have a flavour of *double entendre* and innuendo it was impossible for her to understand.

She at least now realised that it was for his benefit that she was being groomed, instructed, dressed, and lectured by Lady Birchington for hours every day.

She also realised, and it rather amused her, that Lady Birchington was surprised at the correctness of her behaviour at the table, at her good manners, and by the way she could talk without being embarrassed or tongue-tied to Lord Birchington when he was at home.

She was not aware that Kitty's husband had said to her:

"Nice woman, that new friend of yours. Good mannered and intelligent. Pity more of your friends are not out of the same stable."

"I am glad you like her, George," Kitty answered demurely.

"She is sensible, which is more than I can say of most of the young women one meets these days," Lord Birchington continued. "What is her husband like?"

"I have not seen him for years," Kitty replied, "but he is much older than she is."

"Well, do not let her get into trouble while she is in Paris," Lord Birchington advised. "You cannot trust these French fellows and she is too attractive to be wandering about on her own."

"I will do my best to look after her, George."

At the same time Kitty had smiled.

It was obvious that Lina listened to what George said to her, and she had brought out the protective instinct in him.

She might, Kitty thought, bring about the same reaction in Fabian.

Only to think of the *Duc* made Kitty want to grind her teeth, clench her hands and cry to the world how much she longed to punish him for ever having left her.

In a way she knew it would be a 'bitter-sweet' revenge if he really was taken with Lina, because she could not help thinking that even to know and be loved by Fabian for a short time was better than never knowing him at all.

Then she told herself she hated him, of course she hated him! And she would never forgive him for growing bored and casting her aside as he had cast every other woman with whom he had a brief, fiery, ecstatic love-affair which inevitably left them weeping.

'This will punish him,' she thought, 'when the *denouement* comes.'

She would take good care it did and when he realised that Lina was nothing but a farmer's daughter decked out to deceive him he would look a fool!

That was something Fabian had never admitted to being in the whole of his life.

Thinking about him at night with George snoring beside her, Kitty would remember how his love had seemed to consume her like a fiery furnace, and she knew that never before had any man been able to evoke such feelings in her, nor would any ever again.

Then it was over and Fabian had gone out of her

life—except that she would never be able to forget. So revenge would be very sweet.

Daisy and Evie were astounded at how cleverly Lina appeared to play the part that was expected of her.

"However perceptive Fabian may think he is, I swear she will deceive him," Evie said.

"I agree with you," Daisy answered, "and we have the advantage of knowing that Fabian is a Frenchman. Any minor short-comings or slips in her behaviour which would be obvious to an Englishman are unlikely to be noticed by him."

"Better not be too certain of that!" Kitty warned. "Fabian was at School in England for a number of years and also went to Oxford. He spends a great deal of time in this country and strangely his great love-affairs, like ours, were with Englishwomen."

"That is true," Evie agreed. "What is important, Kitty, is to see the girl makes no obvious slips in her behaviour which Fabian will be aware of."

It was extraordinary, Kitty was thinking, how few mistakes Lina did make, and what pleased her was that the girl was intelligent enough to ask when she did not know.

Although she had not been given an explanation why she was being taken to Paris and told to pretend she was a married woman, Lina thought instinctively that in some way The Three Beauties, which was how she thought of Kitty, Daisy, and Evie, were planning to punish the *Duc*.

What he had done and why they should want to do such a thing she could not fathom.

She only knew it was essential from their point of

view that she should play her part convincingly and that he should believe she was Lady Littleton and had spent all her married life isolated in the North of England.

"It will explain why you are so ignorant of social affairs and important people," Kitty said.

She paused before she went on:

"You live on your husband's estate in Yorkshire where he owns a fine family house and is a loved and respected landlord."

"Am I supposed to be rich?" Lina asked.

"Rich enough to be able to afford the sort of clothes you are now wearing," Kitty replied, "and your father was also titled. Now—let me see—what shall we say your name was before you were married?"

She did not wait for Lina to answer, but said:

"Combe will do. I once knew some Combes who lived in Yorkshire, and they can have been neighbours of your husband's."

For a moment Lina nearly said it would be a mistake to be called by her real name.

Then she thought that actually Combe was not an uncommon name, and she had always known she had a great number of relatives scattered all over the British Isles.

It did however seem a strange coincidence that Lady Birchington in making up a story about her past should actually have chosen what was her real name.

Then she thought it was really very funny, and it was a pity she would have to keep it to herself.

Later it would make a good story, she thought, but aloud she said:

"I think Combe is a pretty name."

"Then do not forget it," Kitty admonished, "but unless you are pressed it is better not to talk about yourself. There are so many pitfalls and anyway men only want you to talk about them."

Lina thought with a smile that was certainly true.

All her father's friends when they came to the Castle invariably talked about themselves, the birds they had shot, the fish they had caught, the races they had won.

She found too that Lord Birchington when she asked him questions was delighted that she listened to all he had to say.

The night before they were leaving for Paris Kitty Birchington had a small dinner-party.

The guests were the Marchioness and the Countess, and as the husbands of neither of them were free, two men were specially invited because Kitty wanted to hear their opinion of Lina.

Wearing a gown that had belonged originally to Evie, her hair arranged in a style which made her look very elegant besides being lovely, Lina was an undisputed success.

She had already been clever enough to realise that it was a great mistake to talk too much because she knew she must disguise her past.

She listened therefore to her dinner partners in the same attentive way she always listened to her father, which her mother had told her many years ago was what men expected of a young girl.

"I want you to have opinions of your own," her mother had said, "but darling, do not force them on other people. Far too many women forget that their real important role in life is to be a good listener, and a man is far more easily inspired by a woman when she listens than when she lectures him."

"How can she inspire him if she does not tell him what he ought to do?" Lina had asked and her mother had laughed.

"When a man loves a woman and he admires her, she brings out what is best in him. And no man, or woman for that matter, can give more than they are capable of giving."

Lina thought this over and understood what her mother was trying to say.

"You will inspire many men, I know, darling, in the years to come," her mother had gone on, "just by being yourself. And remember it is always easier to guide a man than drive him."

It was something Lina had thought over after her mother's death and had known she was right.

So she listened attentively to what the gentlemen on either side of her at dinner had to say and had an idea that later in the Drawing-Room, when they talked to Lady Birchington in a low voice that she was not supposed to hear they were praising her.

"The most attractive and intelligent young woman I have met in years!" one of the gentlemen was saying to Kitty. "What is her husband like?"

"Old and rather a bore," Kitty replied.

She saw her guest's eyes light up and was not surprised when he said:

"I hope when you return from Paris, Kitty, you will invite me to dinner again and perhaps I could take you and Lady Littleton to the Theatre."

The gentleman sitting on Lina's other side was far more fulsome in his praise.

"Where on earth did you discover her, Kitty?" he asked. "You will not believe it, but I have a feeling I am falling in love."

"Why not, D'Arcy?" Kitty had asked. "It is something you have done all your life at regular intervals."

"I know, I know!" he replied, "but I have a feeling this will be different, and I am too old to suffer the pangs of misery in pursuing a woman who is far too young for me."

"Then you must leave her alone," Kitty admonished but she knew he had no intention of obeying her.

"You have been a great success," Kitty later said to Lina.

The dinner was over and Kitty and Lina were going upstairs together while Lord Birchington remained behind for a last night-cap.

"Thank you," Lina replied. "Everybody has been very kind to me and it is impossible for me to find the right words in which to thank you."

"You have a long way to go before you need do that," Kitty said. "The real test comes tomorrow."

"Yes, I know," Lina replied, "and I shall pray very hard tonight that I will not fail you."

"That is certainly a good idea," Kitty said lightly. "We need all the assistance we can get, whether it comes from above or below."

This was the sort of remark that would have made the rest of the party at dinner scream with laughter, but Lina only looked a little puzzled.

When she went to her own bedroom she wondered

as she had wondered so often these last few days why exactly she had to act this masquerade and what Lady Birchington and her friends had to gain by it.

'I wish they would tell me the truth,' she thought to herself.

Then when she got into bed after she had been helped to undress by one of the housemaids she told herself she was being very ungrateful.

When she left home she had never for one moment guessed that she would walk into an adventure of this sort.

Instead of lying in a comfortable bed with several trunks packed with the most alluring gowns she could possibly imagine, she might instead be looking after some naughty, obstreperous children, berated by an irate mother for not keeping them under better control.

"I have been so lucky, so very, very lucky!" Lina told herself and she added the little prayer of thankfulness that she had said every night since she came to Belgrave Square.

Nevertheless there was just a little flicker of fear within her which would not be subdued and she knew the reason for it was Fabian, the *Duc* de Saverne.

It had taken some time, but gradually she had realised that the masquerade which was to take place concerned the *Duc* who was to be their host at the Ball on Saturday night.

And it was he about whom The Three Beauties spoke so much, and who they expected to be interested in her, but for what reason Lina could not understand.

'There must be hundreds of women in France to amuse him,' she thought to herself.

When she was trying on the clothes which Kitty had given her and which were being altered by the seamstress, she had suddenly had the terrible thought that perhaps Fabian, whose name seemed invariably to crop up in the conversation whenever The Three Beauties were together, was some horrible, repulsive man like Sir Hector.

She could not imagine where the idea came from, but it struck her that perhaps she was being taken to France so that he would desire her in the same way as Sir Hector.

If that was so, why must she pretend to be a married woman with a husband?

Lina puzzled over this problem for a long time, when after lying awake half the night worrying about it she had been brave enough to ask Kitty:

"Is the gentleman about whom you talk and who is called Fabian also the *Duc* de Saverne whose Ball we are attending on Saturday night?"

"Yes, of course! I thought you realised that!" Kitty answered sharply.

"Is he . . . an . . . old man?"

"Old?" Kitty exclaimed. "No, of course not! Whatever made you think such a thing?"

"I thought perhaps if he was a *Duc* . . ." Lina answered lamely.

"Fabian inherited when he was twenty," Kitty answered, "and that was nearly fourteen years ago."

Lina gave a little sigh of relief, then still curious she said:

"I suppose the *Duc* is married and his wife will be giving the Ball with him."

Kitty laughed.

"I see you have a very imaginative mind," she said. "No, the *Duc* de Saverne is unmarried, although a great number of women on both sides of the Channel have tried to lead him to the altar."

There was a pause, then Kitty went on almost as if she had no wish to offer any further information:

"The *Duc* is giving a Ball for his youngest sister who has just become engaged to be married. Not that he needs a reason to entertain his friends."

Lady Birchington's answers made everything that was happening seem more incomprehensible to Lina than it was already.

If the *Duc* was giving the Ball and was comparatively young and of such social importance, he was hardly likely to notice her among the crowd of friends from both France and England who were to be present.

And yet she knew she was being dressed up and had been given a new name, a title, and a wedding-ring, just in order to play a charade that was to deceive the *Duc*.

"Fabian has the eye of a hawk where a woman is concerned."

"Fabian says a woman's voice is a very important part of her attractions."

"Fabian says that a beautiful woman should glide over a floor, not put her feet down as if she was tramping over the moors."

Every time they said a sentence of this sort to one another, which Lina had soon learnt was really an instruction for her own behaviour, she found herself more and more bewildered.

If she was to play a charade for an audience of one, she could not help wondering what would happen if Fabian failed to applaud as they expected and merely ignored her.

'I suppose in that case I shall be sent home in disgrace,' she thought unhappily.

Then she remembered the £100 she had placed in a Bank in Piccadilly under her own name and which was her own to keep whether things went right or wrong when they reached Paris.

In the meanwhile she was not quite certain what Lady Birchington and her friends would consider right.

It was obvious to Lina that they expected the *Duc* to be attracted to her. Why then must she pretend to be married?

She knew this was going to be the most difficult part of her performance, to talk about the husband who was supposed to be fishing in Scotland instead of accompanying her to Paris.

"I do not understand," she said over and over again to herself.

Yet somehow it was impossible to put into words what she was wanting to know and she was unable therefore to ask Lady Birchington or either of her friends.

To be honest Lina was a little afraid of all of them, especially Lady Birchington.

She had heard the way she spoke to the new maid whom she had managed to procure from Mrs. Hunt's Bureau.

"If you are with me," she said to Lina, "I shall not mind having a maid who does not speak French. Be-

71

sides, I am beginning to realise it is almost impossible to find one. It is extraordinary how uneducated the lower classes are in this country."

"You know I will do anything for you that I can in Paris," Lina said.

"I am sure you will," Kitty replied, "and that means when it concerns shopping you can take the maid with you and get me everything I want."

"Yes, I would love to do that."

Mrs. Hunt had sent to her a maid who had been, Kitty said, in some of the best houses and had only left her last employment because the lady had died.

She was a rather nervous woman and almost as soon as she arrived Lina felt sorry for her.

"I will help you if you have too much to do," she had said when the maid came to her room with a message.

The maid looked at her in astonishment.

"That's very kind of you, M'Lady."

"I know it will be a rush getting off to Paris," Lina said, "so if you tell me when you have too much on your hands I will do what I can."

She smiled before she added:

"Actually I can sew quite well, and I used to help make my own clothes."

She very nearly put this into the present tense, then realised it was a pitfall and changed it at the last moment.

'I must be careful,' she thought. 'Lady Birchington will be very angry if my disguise is not perfect by the time we reach Paris.'

When the maid, whose name was Smith, had been engaged, Lina knew from the way Lady Birchington talked to her and the sharp manner in which she ordered her about that she, Lina, had had a lucky escape.

At the same time she could see that Smith was irritating in many ways and always muddled the orders she was given.

But Lina helped her whenever she could, and she knew that by the time they left for Paris Smith was not only very grateful, but had begun to rely on her help.

The way in which they travelled and which of course Lady Birchington and her friends took for granted intrigued and also amused Lina.

A whole private coach was engaged for them when they reached Calais and this, Lina learned, was on the instructions of the *Duc*.

The three lady's-maids and Lord Birchington's valet were in a carriage to themselves, while the rest of the party had a comfortable Drawing-Room with stewards to wait on them and even sleepers in which they could lie down and take a nap if they wished before they reached the Gare du Nord.

"It is very luxurious," Lina wanted to say.

But she kept her remarks to herself knowing that the people with whom she was travelling took such comfort as a matter of course.

She had been surprised to find that Lord Birchington was the only male member of their party, but she learned from the general conversation that the Marquess of Holme and the Earl of Pendock found Paris a bore if they had to be accompanied by their wives.

Both of them, for no reason that Lina could understand, disliked the *Duc*.

The conversation on the train from London to Dover, and again from Calais to Paris was all about people whom Lina did not know, and The Three Beauties related scandalous anecdotes about their friends which made them laugh a little spitefully.

Because the unpleasant way in which they were talking somehow spoiled the dream-like quality of the journey, Lina changed her place so that she could look out of the window and watched the countryside flash past.

Northern France was exactly as she had expected it to be: flat with a lack of hedges which seemed very strange after the high hedgerows of England.

The cypress trees which bordered the roads and the colours of the fields with their various crops, made a patchwork that she thought had a beauty all of its own.

As the light faded she could see her reflection in the window and found it hard to recognise herself in the extremely elegant travelling-gown which had belonged to the Countess of Pendock.

Her hat trimmed with ostrich feathers of the same colour seemed to Lina to be a height of elegance which she had never expected to attain.

She also realised that she was wearing the clothes of a married woman, and not those of a young girl.

Even after five days she still found it strange to wear a wedding-ring on the third finger of her left hand, and whenever she took her gloves off she felt it winked at her almost like a warning light at sea.

'I wonder what will happen in Paris?' she thought as the train sped on through the dusk.

The cypress trees now seemed to point like dark fingers towards the first stars coming out overhead.

Lina felt a tremor of fear, but whether it was because she was afraid of what she would find in Paris, or because she was afraid she would fail Lady Birchington's trust in her, she was not sure.

Then she told herself once again that nobody could be so lucky as to have the fantastic experience of being taken to Paris, and she would never in her wildest dreams have thought she would ever have enough money to afford to go abroad.

She remembered the things her mother had talked about: the Palace of Versailles, the Seine, the pictures in the Louvre, the Arc de Triomphe, the Place Vendôme with a statue of Napoleon on a high column.

'I shall see them all!' Lina thought with a little thrill of excitement.

She could never be grateful enough to Lady Birchington for giving her the chance of coming on this journey.

Then like a menacing shadow passing over her anticipation of what lay ahead she remembered the *Duc*.

"Why must I act this part to deceive him?" she asked herself yet again.

She had guessed by this time that Lady Birchington and her friends were playing some kind of trick on him, but she could not imagine what they expected to gain from it.

Last night she had found it difficult to sleep because she was so excited about going to France, but also because she felt uneasy at what she could only describe to herself as a real fear that the *Duc* in meeting her would immediately be aware that she was acting a part.

Lady Birchington had told her what she should say to him.

"If the *Duc* asks you about your home and your husband, you must say as little as possible. Question him about himself. Flatter him, tell him you have heard of his distinction and the treasures he possesses."

"You have already told me about his houses and his vast estates," Lina said.

"Ask him to tell you about his pictures."

"Can you remember some of the famous ones he owns?"

Kitty had shaken her head.

"Pictures bore me," she said, "but I know Fabian's collection is unique. Just ask him to describe them to you."

Lina wanted to ask if the *Duc* would not find this a bore.

It seemed to her extraordinary that she should be taken to Paris to talk to a man who was obviously very distinguished and a socialite about his pictures and his possessions when she had not the slightest idea what they were.

'There must be other things that interest him,' she thought a little despairingly and enquired:

"Does the *Duc* own any horses?"

"Of course he does!" Kitty replied. "He won the Grand Prix last year."

Lina was aware this was a famous horse-race, and she thought that if the *Duc* were an English owner it would have been easy to look him up in the Sporting Paper her father took every week.

Unfortunately she knew nothing about French horses or the names of the French newspapers which would tell her about them.

"Will you tell me about the *Duc*?" she had asked a little hesitatingly last night when she and her hostess were walking upstairs before dinner.

"What do you want to know?" Kitty asked sharply.

"As he is our host on Saturday night, and I think, although I may be wrong, I am acting this part especially for him, I feel I should know more about him than I do at the moment."

"There is no need for that," Kitty replied. "You will find out everything you want to know when you get to France. Now hurry and change, or you will be late for dinner."

She went to her own bedroom as she spoke and inexplicably slammed the door.

Lina was aware that she must have said something wrong but why her hostess was annoyed she had no idea.

'I shall just have to try and find out things for myself.'

She thought the same when darkness came and a very short while later the train steamed into the Gare du Nord.

77

Lina had already learnt that the *Duc* had arranged where his English friends would stay when they reached Paris.

What she had expected was a Hotel.

Instead she had learned that she and Lord and Lady Birchington were to stay with one of the *Duc*'s cousins in a house on the Champs Élysées, while the Marchioness and the Countess were to be the guests of the *Duc*'s aunt who had a huge mansion on the edge of the Bois.

"I dare say we shall be a larger party, Kitty," the Marchioness said. "At the same time, it is a bore to be on the outskirts of Paris rather than inside. I envy you being with the *Comtesse* de la Tour."

"I am a little apprehensive," Kitty replied, "as to what Yvonne will think of Lina."

Daisy's eyebrows had been raised for a moment. Then she laughed.

"I see what you mean," she said. "You do not think she will like the competition."

"She resented me," Kitty said. "Now she thinks my teeth are drawn where Fabian is concerned, but I have the uncomfortable feeling that with Lina it will be a different 'kettle of fish'!"

"Do you mean to tell me," Evie asked, "that Yvonne is still trying to marry Fabian?"

"Of course she is!" Kitty replied. "She has been in love with him for years and was quite certain he would succumb to family pressure sooner or later and marry her because they would make a very suitable couple. What is more, their lands adjoin on one side of Fabian's estate."

"That is what I call typically French reasoning," Daisy scoffed.

"It happens in every country," Evie said. "My mother-in-law tried for years to marry Arthur to a hideous old harridan because they were neighbours, and their boundaries adjoined in Shropshire."

"So I am not particularly looking forward to Yvonne's reaction when she sees Lina," Kitty said.

"If you ask me she is a fool to run after Fabian. It will only make him run in the opposite direction."

Lina could hear the conversation that was taking place on the other side of the carriage, but she deliberately tried not to listen.

It only worried her when she attempted to fit the jig-saw puzzle of things which The Three Beauties said to each other in conversation together with names and people.

She had learned in the last five days since she had been in Belgrave Square to appear to be attentive and to listen to what was being said while at the same time allowing her mind to slip away to things she found more interesting.

There were books in Lord Birchington's Study which she longed to find time to read, and there were pictures in the Drawing-Room and on the stairs which she learned he had inherited and which she found fascinating to look at.

But she soon learned that Kitty knew nothing about them.

As she herself was so well-educated, she was rapidly coming to the conclusion, and she felt it was rather revealing, that the three beautiful women who were sponsoring this strange charade in which she was taking part were interested only in themselves.

Her mother had always said that the girls from important families in Society were dragged up with only a spattering of knowledge, and when they finally made their debut were actually ignorant to the point of absurdity.

"And yet, dearest, it is a strange phenomenon," she said, "that they become the sophisticated, beautiful women who grace the Drawing-Rooms of London, and to whom every man bows in admiration."

She gave a little sigh before she went on:

"I have always thought it unfair that a man has a very comprehensive education at School and University, while women are supposed to be content with their lives as long as they are wives and mothers."

"I think Papa has always appreciated the fact that you know so much and are so well read," Lina remarked.

Her mother had laughed.

"If you are asking me if your father married me for my brains, the answer is 'no'. But I promise you, it has made our lives together so much more enjoyable because we have so many interests in common to discuss and argue about."

Because they had been so happy Lina could understand her father's sense of loss when her mother had died.

She had realised it vaguely at first, then more perceptively that he was not the sort of man who ingratiated himself with his neighbours, and that it was not he, but her mother who had been popular.

When he had started gambling and seemed to prefer the company of Sir Hector, their friends had found it easier to drop the invitations that might have been sent to him with a shrug of their shoulders and say it was a pity he had 'gone to the Devil'.

'It is not fair on Papa,' Lina often thought, but there was nothing she could do about it, and she was aware that in consequence because he was isolated from their neighbours, so was she.

Now she was going to a Ball in Paris and she was sure that, although she was going in very strange circumstances and acting some sort of part, her mother would be pleased that she would see the Social World that her circumstances had denied her.

'If only Mama could be here it would be wonderful!' Lina thought as she looked out into the darkness.

She thought how her mother would have been able to reveal the beauties of Paris to her, and because she was so well read she would doubtless have known the histories of the great French families whom the *Duc* would entertain at his Ball, families which had survived the Revolution and others created by Napoleon, which however important they had become were still not accepted by the *Ancien Régime*.

'I am sure there will be some books where we are staying which will give me the chance to read about the people I will meet,' Lina thought.

Because the idea excited her, she ceased to listen to the conversation that was taking place on the other side of the carriage.

Instead her imagination carried her away into the past and she knew this was not only a journey of pleasure but also one of exploration that she would remember all her life.

Chapter Four

KITTY AND Lina stepped out of the carriage and walked into the house, while footmen followed with a pile of cardboard boxes acquired while they were out shopping.

To Lina it had been a fascinating experience not only to enter what she knew were the best shops in Paris, but also to see somebody spending money in a manner that made her gasp.

She thought it impossible that Kitty would ever need all the gloves, sunshades, shoes, bags, and other accessories she had purchased, and as she watched wide-eyed she wondered if the day would ever come when she could shop in the same profligate manner.

She was sure that it was very unlikely.

As they drove back towards the Champs Élysées Kitty said:

"I was talking to my friends last night, and we decided it would sound strange if you did not call us by our Christian names. Of course, it is something you will cease to do immediately we return to London."

"Yes, of course," Lina replied.

She thought with a little smile that it was obviously an effort for Kitty to suggest such a thing.

She was, in fact, aware without their having said anything that The Three Beauties still thought of her as having the same status, or what they would describe as 'class', as either the lady's-maid or the Governess she had aspired to be.

"Or for that matter the daughter of a farmer," Lina said to herself and thought how angry her father would be at being described in such terms.

It was really rather humiliating, she thought, that her ancestry, of which her father and mother had been so proud, had to be displayed on a Family Tree rather than that people should be aware of it when they met her.

Yet in some strange way she thought that she had been brought to Paris, because The Three Beauties thought of her as an inferior.

She could not however put it into words, so she decided the best thing to do would be to stop worrying and accept everything as it come, especially the joy of seeing Paris.

It had been thrilling to see the Place de la Concorde, and when they drove into the Place Vendôme she thought it was exactly what she had expected, except that everything in Paris seemed to have a magic of its own.

As they reached the hall the *Maître des Chambres* who was waiting for them, said to Kitty:

"Pardon, Madame, but *le Coiffeur* has been here for some time."

Kitty gave a little cry of horror.

"I had forgotten I had asked Alexandre to come before luncheon. Go upstairs at once Lina, and let him start on your hair before I join you."

Because there was an urgency in Kitty's voice and because Lina had already learnt that a French *Coiffeur* had a very special place in the social world because no woman could do without him, she ran up the stairs.

Smith had obviously anticipated she would be first, for she found a thin, aesthetic-looking Frenchman already in her bedroom looking out of the window and tapping a comb impatiently on the palm of his hand.

"I am so sorry, *Monsieur* Alexandre," Lina said in her perfect Parisian French, "but Lady Birchington and I forgot the time and we can only apologise most sincerely for keeping you waiting."

Alexandre looked at her and it was obvious that it was not so much her words that pleased him, but her appearance.

"Vous êtes Lady Littleton?" he asked.

"Yes," Lina replied, "and please try to make me look very smart and elegant. I am afraid that living as I do in the country in England, my hair has been sadly neglected."

She took off her hat and jacket as she spoke and Alexandre put over her shoulders a white muslin cape.

Then she sat down on the stool in front of the dressing-table and he undid her hair which she had arranged herself that morning, muttering as he did so, in a disparaging manner which made her want to laugh.

Her very fair hair was as fine and delicate as silk, and when it fell over her shoulders, it reached almost to her waist.

"How can you have distorted and misused anything so exquisite in such a horrible manner?" Alexandre questioned dramatically.

"I am afraid Englishwomen are not so concerned with their hair as the French," Lina smiled.

Alexandre threw up his hands to exclaim:

"Les Anglaises! C'est incroyable!"

He took a hair-brush and started with long, smooth strokes to brush Lina's hair until it seemed to dance in the air as if it had an independent life all of its own.

Then he put down the brush and said:

"Alors, we must decide. Do you, My Lady, wish your hair to be arranged in the present fashion with a small knot on top of your head? Or would you wish me to try a new style, one that has only just been introduced to Paris and will certainly not have reached England."

"I do not know what to say," Lina replied.

Then she suddenly thought that this was a question she must ask Kitty. After so much trouble had been taken over her gowns in which she had had no say whatsoever, she was quite certain Kitty would have very definite ideas on how her hair should be dressed.

Impulsively she jumped up from the stool.

"Wait one moment, *Monsieur!*" she said. "I will just ask Lady Birchington which she would prefer. She will be angry if we do not make the right choice."

She smiled at him beguilingly and felt that he understood her predicament as she ran from the room and across the corridor to Kitty's bedroom.

To her surprise Kitty was not there and Smith said she had not yet come upstairs.

'She must still be writing her note,' Lina thought.

She ran down into the Hall and opened the door of the Salon where Kitty had gone when they arrived back at the house.

She saw Kitty at the far end of the room and hurried towards her saying:

"I must ask your advice. Alexandre says that he can arrange my hair in a new way which has not yet been seen in Paris, but I am frightened you might not approve."

Only as she reached Kitty who was standing up did she realise that she was not alone and that there was somebody with her.

A man was sitting in an armchair which had its back to the door and he rose to his feet.

"I can quite see," he said, speaking in English with just a faint accent, "that this is a world-shattering problem!"

Lina had given a little gasp of surprise when she had first realised he was there.

Now as she turned to look at him she knew without being told that this was Fabian, the *Duc* de Saverne, about whom she had heard so much.

He looked exactly as she might have expected.

Not very tall, but slim, elegant, and in a way she could not describe almost aggressively masculine.

He had thick dark hair, and while he was not really handsome he had a strange, unforgettable face which made him look different from any man Lina had ever seen before.

Nobody could have mistaken him for being of any other nationality than French and his black eyes seemed to twinkle and his lips to curve with a mocking smile which made Lina in a strange way, feel she knew him.

He was somebody she had imagined but never expected to meet in real life.

She was suddenly aware of how unconventional she must look in the white cape with her hair hanging over her shoulders.

She gave Kitty a nervous little smile.

"I am sorry . . . I apologise," she said. "I thought you were . . . alone."

"I have a caller, Lina," Kitty replied. "Let me introduce you to the *Duc* de Saverne, your host of tomorrow evening! Fabian, this is Lady Littleton who I told you I was bringing with me."

"*Enchanté, Madame,*" the *Duc* said and held out his hand.

As Lina put her hand in his he raised it and she felt that there was a vibration about his fingers that seemed to echo the twinkle in his eyes.

'He is quite overwhelming and very, very sure of himself,' she thought.

Then she hastily took her hand from his and said to Kitty:

"Forgive . . . me."

She would have turned away but the *Duc* said:

"Wait! We have not yet decided how your hair shall be arranged, and may I add it looks very lovely as it is now."

"It is hardly the way she could appear at a Ball," Kitty remarked sharply.

"No, of course not," the *Duc* agreed, "but give Alexandre my congratulations. He has found a perfect model for his new style, and I shall be waiting impatiently to see it."

"The *Duc* is right, Lina," Kitty said, "so tell Alexandre what to do."

She did not say any more, but Lina was aware that she was dismissed, and largely because Kitty wanted to be alone with the *Duc*.

"Thank you," she said.

She was determined only to look at Kitty, but she was acutely aware that the *Duc* was watching her.

She went from the room and as she hurried up the stairs she had the feeling she was breathless not with the speed at which she was climbing them, but because she had met the man for whom she had been brought to Paris.

While Alexandre was arranging her hair Lina found herself thinking of the *Duc* and wondering what he had thought of her.

She was also apprehensive in case Kitty should be angry because she had burst into the Salon without having first made certain that she was alone.

"That will be a black mark against me," she told herself.

Strangely enough, a little later, just as Alexandre was putting the finishing touches to her hair, Kitty came upstairs and seemed to be in a very good mood.

She praised Alexandre's efforts and certainly Lina's hair was very different from the way it had ever looked before.

She realised herself that it not only framed her face, but the new style became what the poets called a 'crowning glory'.

Only when they were having luncheon at a late hour and she and Kitty were alone as their hostess had another appointment did Lina say humbly:

"I am sorry . . . I disturbed you this morning. I had no idea there would be . . . anybody with you."

"Well, now you have met the *Duc*," Kitty answered, "what do you think of him?"

"He is . . . magnificent . . . and I suppose . . ."

Kitty gave her a sharp glance.

"Every woman thinks that. But I am hoping you will not make a fool of yourself over him."

Lina looked at Kitty in surprise, who went on:

"You told me at our first interview that you were a good girl, and now I have brought you to Paris I advise you not to forget the principles with which you have been brought up."

Lina felt the colour come into her face.

"I would never think of . . . doing anything . . . wrong," she declared, "if that is what you are . . . suggesting!"

Once again she remembered the servants in the Park and the ugly expression in Sir Hector's eyes which had frightened her.

Because she suddenly felt insulted by Kitty's insinuation she said:

"I cannot imagine why you should think I might behave...badly with the *Duc* or with any...other man, and if you cannot...trust me I think I should go back to...England today without...attending the Ball."

She knew as she spoke it would almost break her heart if Kitty accepted her suggestion.

At the same time a pride she had not realised she possessed told her she must answer such ugly suspicions which would have horrified both her mother and her father.

"Of course I trust you," Kitty said quickly. "But it is well known that the *Duc* considers himself irresistible, which is what most women find him—to their cost."

The way Kitty spoke made Lina think she had been very obtuse not to realise that at one time Kitty must have had a flirtation with the *Duc*.

She was not quite certain what this entailed, but she thought such a thing would have been very reprehensible, considering that Kitty was married and had been since she was eighteen.

Then she wondered if the *Duc* had also flirted with Daisy and Evie.

Had they all found him irresistible? She could not believe such a thing was possible.

And yet the way they had talked about him, the fact that he was obviously continually in their thoughts made it clear now that he must have been a very intimate friend.

But they were married, they all had husbands, and

91

Lina could not imagine her mother ever flirting with anybody or even being aware that another man existed while her father was there.

Of course she knew such things happened, and as if her eyes were suddenly opened and she had been very blind until this moment, Lina could now remember things that had been said which had made no sense at the time.

"Fabian can ask the time and make it sound like a caress!"

"Fabian can make a plain woman feel like a Venus."

"Fabian knows he is irresistible, and it would be a lie for any woman to deny it!"

Fabian, always Fabian!

"I am quite certain he is spoilt and conceited," Lina told herself.

She learned when luncheon was over that she was to see the *Duc* again far more quickly than she had expected.

"The *Duc* told me this morning that the decorations have been put up in his Ball-Room," Kitty said, "and he wants me to see them."

"I will wait here until you get back," Lina answered.

"Do not be so ridiculous!" Kitty said sharply. "You are to come with me."

She did not seem very pleased at the idea, but there was nothing Lina could do but go upstairs and change into one of the attractive afternoon gowns that had belonged to Evie.

It had an expensive simplicity about it, and when Lina put on the hat that went with it she thought no one would believe that she had been married for five years as Lady Littleton was supposed to have been.

Kitty gave her an appraising glance as she went downstairs but as she did not comment Lina imagined she must have passed muster.

The *Duc*'s house was so near that it would have been quite easy to walk, especially as it was a sunny afternoon, but an open carriage was waiting for them and they arrived in style.

"May I say how delighted I am to see you again, Lady Littleton," the *Duc* said as he greeted them in the Hall.

He kissed first Kitty's hand, and Lina noticed that his lips actually touched her glove.

She had learned from *Madame* de Beauvais who had taught her French, that the usual greeting from a Frenchman was only a perfunctory gesture.

This therefore confirmed what she already suspected, that the *Duc* and Kitty had once had a flirtation.

Lina thought she was not really surprised.

There was no doubt that Lady Birchington was very beautiful and this afternoon she looked lovelier than usual with her eyes looking up into the *Duc*'s and her red hair glinting in the sunshine.

"Now, Kitty, I want your advice," the *Duc* was saying, "and yours, Lady Littleton. I want the Ball to be sensational."

As he spoke he started to walk from the Hall along the wide corridor which was furnished with the most magnificent Louis XV commodes and inlaid marble tables.

The walls were hung with portraits of the de Saverne ancestors.

Lina was fascinated, and because Kitty was talking softly and intimately to the *Duc* it gave her the chance to look around her thinking she must remember everything she saw and store it away in her mind.

"I shall never have the chance of seeing such treasures again," she told herself.

How fortunate it was she was able to see the *Duc's* house before it was packed with people!

The Ball-Room which was built out at the end of the house and opened onto the garden was large, architecturally distinguished, and the *Duc* had made it sensational.

Instead of the garlands of flowers which Lina had read were the usual decorations for a Ball-Room, it had been transformed into a replica of Venice.

There were paintings on the walls depicting San Marco and when they looked out of the window of the Ball-Room Kitty gave a shriek of excitement!

The garden had been turned into a lake on which there were gondolas, and at one end of it there was a replica of the Bridge of Sighs.

"Fabian!" she exclaimed, "I have never seen anything so fascinating!"

"I always meant to give a Ball in Venice," he said, "but it would be too far to take my friends like you. So I thought if we could not go to Venice, the obvious solution was to bring Venice to Paris!"

"It is not only an intriguing idea," Kitty said, "but very, very romantic!"

She looked at the *Duc* from under her eye-lashes as she spoke, but saw he was looking at Lina.

Kitty's lips tightened.

Then as if she forced herself to do so she walked through one of the windows of the Ball-Room as if she intended to inspect the garden.

"What do you think of it, Lady Littleton?" the *Duc* asked.

"I have always dreamed of going to Venice," Lina replied, "so seeing this is like being in my dreams, only more wonderful."

The *Duc* smiled.

"Wait until you see it at night when the lanterns have been lit and the gondolas move on the lake, and we dance to the music of a hundred violins."

"I can only hope I will not die before tomorrow night," Lina exclaimed and he laughed.

"I am sure you will not do that and, who knows, perhaps my Venice will teach you to love differently from any way you have loved before."

Lina did not look at him questioningly as he thought any other woman would have done.

Instead she said as if she was following her own train of thought:

"Where Venice sate in state, throned on her hundred isles!"

"So you know your Byron!"

"Yes, of course!" Linda replied, "and tomorrow night I shall be able to say as he did:

"I stood in Venice, on the Bridge of Sighs; A palace and a prison on each hand."

95

"Not a prison," the *Duc* said, "unless of course it is the prison every woman seeks."

There was a little pause before Lina realised he was waiting for her to reply and she asked:

"What is that?"

"The prison of love, Lady Littleton."

For the first time since they had come into the Ball-Room Lina looked at him.

There was an expression in his dark eyes that startled her.

'He is trying to flirt with me,' she thought, 'and that is something that they anticipated he would do.'

She looked away from him and walked towards the window.

"Tell me," she said, "how you made an artificial lake without spoiling the garden? It must have been quite an engineering feat."

She stepped through the window as she spoke and found herself on a terrace which overlooked the water and it was where Kitty was standing, staring, Lina thought, at the Bridge of Sighs.

"I am sure we should congratulate the *Duc* on a very ingenious idea," she said as Lina joined her.

"I am asking how it has been achieved," Lina replied.

"Lady Littleton is interested more in the operation than the result," the *Duc* remarked and Lina thought he was mocking her.

"Tomorrow night everybody will find it very romantic," Kitty said. "I know I shall!"

"There is no need to wait until tomorrow for romance," the *Duc* replied. "Pierre de Castlenagne has been counting the days until you arrive and has suggested that tonight we dine at his house under the stars. I will try to explain to Lady Littleton how they manage to remain in the firmament without falling down!"

"I am sure Lina will find that fascinating!" Kitty said sarcastically.

"Then shall we say eight o'clock?" the *Duc* asked.

"Of course we would love it," Kitty said, "but I am afraid George cannot join us. He has a previous engagement with a man with whom he wishes to discuss horses."

She gave a little laugh before she added:

"Only George would come to Paris to talk about horses!"

"I know that," the *Duc* replied. "I met the noble Earl a short while ago at the Traveller's Club, and he told me where he was going this evening."

"Then you were quite certain that Lina and I would accept your invitation!" Kitty questioned lightly.

"I was convinced you would not be so unkind as to refuse me."

Lina thought that she might be listening to a play.

She and one of her teachers had often read plays to each other, taking different parts and trying to make the various characters sound different and convincing.

But the repartee between Kitty and the *Duc* was the real thing and Lina found it fascinating.

It was almost as if they crossed swords with each other, and she had an idea they were duelling, although what they were fighting over she had no idea.

She looked over the balustrade and thought the sunlit water was very lovely.

She could see the lake was quite shallow in the daylight and looked artificial, but the gondolas seemed real and she wondered if the *Duc* had brought them from Venice or if he had been able to buy or hire them in Paris.

She wanted to ask him questions but thought he would mock at her.

He would obviously expect everyone to say the scene he had created was very romantic and not to be interested in the mechanics of how it was achieved.

"I must listen and not talk," Lina told herself.

But she knew it was going to be difficult because there were so many things about which she was curious.

They only stayed for a short while, then Kitty said they had other things to do and anyway they had arranged to meet Daisy and Evie.

"It was so delightful to see them again," the *Duc* remarked.

"You have already seen them?" Kitty asked sharply.

"I called on them this morning before they left on a shopping expedition which is every woman's preoccupation when she comes to Paris."

"I am disappointed that you did not call on me first," Kitty pouted.

"I wanted to bring you here, but the workmen had not finished until luncheontime," the *Duc* replied.

Lina was aware that Kitty was pleased with his answer and once again he was kissing their hands.

Then they were driving away in the carriage which was waiting for them.

"There are some more things I have to buy," Kitty said as if an explanation was needed as they drove towards the Place de la Concorde.

Lina did not answer and after a moment Kitty asked:

"Well, what do you think of the *Duc* and his house?"

"He must be very, very rich!"

"He is!"

"I suppose some people would be shocked at him for spending so much money on a Ball which, after all, will only last for one night."

"That is a very tiresome remark," Kitty snapped, "and not the sort of thing that Fabian or anybody else will want to hear! If you have the socialistic ideas of the Countess of Warwick, all I can say is that you will very quickly bore Fabian with your theories, as she bored the Prince of Wales."

Lina was astonished. Then she said quickly:

"I am...sorry. I will not say...anything like...that again."

"I should hope not," Kitty said. "Men only want women to be complacent and charming and, if you have a brain, keep it hidden because they are not going to appreciate it!"

Lina felt crushed.

At the same time she remembered her mother had said that a man wanted a woman to listen and not talk, and she had therefore been very foolish.

"I am...sorry," she said again, "I will be very, very careful in future."

99

"I should hope so," Kitty said. "It has cost a great deal of money and taken up a lot of my time to bring you here. The least you can do is to play the part allotted to you intelligently."

Lina longed to reply that she had just told her not to be intelligent.

Then she told herself she must do as she was told and not expect them to explain exactly what was happening.

However, when they arrived back at the house after shopping to find Daisy and Evie waiting for them, Kitty became good-tempered and was ready to boast of what a success Lina had been.

"We are both dining with him tonight," she said. "He made the excuse that Pierre was looking forward to seeing me, but I am quite certain it was because he wanted to see Lina again."

"Fabian came to see us this morning!" Daisy said.

"Yes, I know," Kitty replied. "He told me! But he took me to see his arrangements for the Ball because he wanted my advice!"

She spoke as if she was deliberately trying to score off her two friends. Then as if she remembered Lina was there she said:

"I am sure things are working out exactly as we intended. But I will tell you more later."

Lina felt sure that Kitty would do this only when she had gone upstairs to take off her hat and gloves.

She deliberately lingered in her bedroom, tidying her hair where it had been slightly crushed by her hat and hoping because of their dinner appointment, that it would keep its shape.

Then a servant knocked on the door to tell her that tea was ready and she went down to the Salon being sure that in her absence The Three Beauties had been talking about her.

There was a sudden silence as she entered the room which told her she was right, and she felt as she walked towards them that they were all regarding her critically, at the same time resentfully, although she was not quite certain why.

The *Comte's* house, which was in the Rue du Faubourg St. Honoré, was smaller than the *Duc's* but very attractive.

It was a warm evening and as the *Duc* had promised they dined in the garden under the trees, with the stars overhead and gold candelabra.

It was undoubtedly, Lina thought, very romantic, but Kitty said so and praised everything before she had a chance to speak.

The *Comte* was a much older man than she had expected, but was delighted to see Kitty and kissed both her hands, one after the other with no pretence about it. Then he said:

"You are even lovelier than I remember, *ma belle*, and I have found it impossible to forget you."

"Why should you want to?" Kitty asked.

"For my own peace of mind, and because you spoil

my pleasure in every other woman who is not as beautiful as you."

Again Lina thought they were speaking like characters in a play and she listened entranced until the *Duc* who had been waiting for them at the *Comte*'s house said:

"Pay some attention to me, Lady Littleton. I want you to tell me about yourself."

"I would rather talk about you," Lina replied. "I was thinking that your family history must be very interesting. Is there a book in which I can read about your ancestors?"

"If you are really interested, I will tell you what you want to know," the *Duc* replied.

"Then please do that," Lina said. "Have you been part of French history for many centuries, and were your ancestors guillotined in the Revolution?"

The *Duc* laughed.

"I never remember before having such questions fired at me the moment I met anybody as enchanting as yourself."

Lina glanced quickly at Kitty, afraid she would be looking at her disapprovingly. Then she asked:

"Is it . . . wrong to be so . . . curious?"

"It is not in the least wrong," the *Duc* replied, "and very flattering but surprising."

"I find history so fascinating," Lina said. "If only I had known earlier I was coming to Paris I could have looked up about the people I should meet, and it would have made it much easier for me to understand them."

"So you want to understand me?"

"Not as a man, but as head of your family, and why you are in that position," Lina replied, without thinking.

Then she realised that again was something she should not have said and looked apprehensively at the *Duc* in case he should think her rude.

"You are a very surprising person, Lady Littleton," he said, "and I am referring to what you say rather than how you look."

"Why?" Lina asked.

"Because looking as you do, I would have imagined you only would hear paeans of praise to your beauty. Instead you tell me you are interested in engineering feats and ghosts from the past! I cannot believe they are more interesting than those who are alive and beside you."

"I am afraid . . . from what you are . . . saying that I have been rather . . . rude," Lina said.

"Not in the slightest," the *Duc* replied. "Only unexpected and let me tell you I enjoy the unexpected because it is something I very rarely find."

"What are your interests?"

She wanted to add, "Apart from women". Then she knew that would indeed be very rude, and Kitty would be furious.

Strangely enough it seemed as if the *Duc* was aware of what she was thinking.

"Shall I promise you," he asked, "that whatever you say to me, however unexpected, I will not think it rude? And will certainly not be offended."

"You are . . . sure of . . . that?"

She looked quickly to where Kitty was deep in conversation of an obviously very private nature with the *Comte* and said:

"You see ... this is all ... new to me and very different from the life I have ... lived before I became Kitty's ... friend."

"Kitty told me that you have been living in the country."

"Yes."

"What made you decide to come to Paris? Have you quarrelled with your husband? Or are you running away from him?"

She was not running away from a husband, Lina thought, but from Sir Hector and he was certainly far more terrifying than any husband could have been.

The *Duc* was watching her and as she did not reply he said:

"So you *were* running away!"

"I have ... not said ... so."

"I can read your thoughts."

"I hope not," Lina said quickly. "And if you can ... it is something you must not do."

"Why not?"

"Because it is an intrusion, and I would not wish anybody to know what I am thinking."

"Are your thoughts so shocking?"

"No, of course not! But they are mine, and if one cannot possess one's thoughts, then one can no longer be oneself."

"I find it very enjoyable, Lady Littleton, to try to read your thoughts. It is something for instance which a man who is in love with you will be able to do very easily."

"I would still want them to myself."

"Love is not like that!" the *Duc* replied.

"Why . . . not?"

"When one is really in love one becomes part of the person one loves. Then there are no divisions, no barriers! Love is overwhelming and completely absorbing."

"I suppose that is . . . true," Lina said, "but I think I would be rather . . . afraid of that sort of love."

She was thinking aloud, and she was startled when he said quickly:

"So you have never been in love?"

Too late Lina remembered the husband who was supposed to be fishing in Scotland who was much older than she was and not particularly interested in her.

She had made a slip, but it would be a mistake to admit it.

"I expect love is the same the world over, but everybody has different ideas about it," she said lightly. "Not everybody experiences the love you are talking about! It may be very different from what I mean by it."

"I doubt if there is any difference," the *Duc* answered, "but it might be definitely exciting to find out."

Chapter Five

WHEN THE dinner was over Kitty and the *Comte* walked casually away into the shadows of the garden.

The servants had removed the Dinner table and instead put a small side-table beside the *Duc* on which he could place his glass of brandy.

They had been sitting during dinner on comfortably cushioned arm-chairs. Now the *Duc* crossed his legs and sat back at his ease, but turned sideways so that he could look at Lina.

"You intrigue me," he said, "but I think, Lady Littleton, that you are not exactly what you appear."

Lina thought this was perceptive of him. At the same time, it was dangerous.

She was quite certain that if he guessed she was taking part in a charade he would be very angry.

"Why... should you... think that?" she asked tentatively.

"For one thing because you look so very young. Kitty tells me you have been married for five years," he answered, "but I do not believe it, unless you were married from the cradle."

Lina laughed.

"You are very flattering, *Monsieur*!"

"Must we be so formal?" the *Duc* asked. "I want to call you Lina. It is a name that suits you, and you glow like the light after which you are named."

"You know my name means 'light'?" Lina enquired.

"Are you accusing me of being an ignoramus?" the *Duc* enquired. "I have had the advantage of an English Public School and an English University."

"Then you were very lucky," Lina said. "In England as I expect you know, it is not considered necessary that girls should be educated."

"Yet you have been!"

"Yes, my mother insisted on it, and although I did not go to school I had some very good teachers, especially the one who taught me French."

"And your husband taught you about love?"

Lina stiffened.

She felt he had no right to speak to her in such a way, and yet for some reason she did not understand she was not affronted, but merely felt shy.

"You are being evasive with me," the *Duc* said as she did not speak. "Why should we not talk of love which is the inevitable conclusion of a conversation between a man and a woman?"

"You are speaking of...French men and French women," Lina managed to say.

"Of French men, perhaps," the *Duc* replied, "but women are feminine whatever nation they belong to."

"Perhaps I am different," Lina said, "but I would much rather talk of . . . other things. You have still not told me about your ancestors."

"My ancestors are dead!" the *Duc* replied, "while I am very much alive. Look at me, Lina. I want you to look at me."

She had a feeling this would be a mistake and instead she turned her face up to the sky saying:

"I think you . . . promised to talk to me . . . about the stars."

"I am not interested in stars at the moment," the *Duc* said, "but in you."

There was something in the way he spoke and in the depths of his voice that made Lina feel a little quiver run through her.

She had been acutely aware of him all through dinner as he sat beside her.

The vibrations she had sensed coming from him when he had first touched her hand had grown in intensity until she felt without moving he reached out towards her and she could not avoid him.

Now she looked down the garden hoping to see Kitty returning with the *Comte* but there was no sign of them and the *Duc* said very quietly:

"I think you are afraid of being alone with me. Why should you feel like that?"

He waited for an answer and after a moment Lina said:

"I told you . . . I have been living . . . very quietly in the country . . . and I am not used to the . . . life you lead."

"What you know about my life is only what you

have heard, and I can imagine all too well what that must be," the *Duc* replied. "Let us forget the past and concentrate on the present."

"Which is very exciting for me," Lina said quickly, "because tomorrow night I shall be attending my first Ball."

There was a pause before the *Duc* said:

"Is that true?"

"I have told you I am a country-cousin."

"You certainly do not look like one."

She knew as he spoke that he was thinking of her clothes, and she wondered what he would say if she told him they were second-hand and had been given to her just for the trip to Paris.

Instead she replied:

"Again we are talking of me when I would much rather talk about you."

"Very well," the *Duc* said. "I will talk about myself, and tell you that when you came into the Salon this morning you not only looked exquisitely beautiful, but I felt as if I had seen you before, and you must therefore have been part of my dreams."

It was what Lina had felt too, but she told herself it was the sort of thing the *Duc* would say to any woman with whom he was trying to flirt.

"I was expecting to meet you for the first time tomorrow night," she said, "when I will be dressed in all my finery for your Ball."

"You could not look more beautiful than you did with your hair over your shoulders," the *Duc* said, "and I have the irresistible desire, Lina, to touch it."

Again there was that deep note in his voice that she felt vibrating within her like a note of music.

"Please," she said quickly, "you must . . . not behave . . . like this."

"Like what?" the *Duc* asked. "What am I doing that is wrong? I am not touching you, although I want to."

"I think," Lina said slowly, "that you are trying to . . . flirt with me, and it is . . . something I should not . . . allow."

" 'Flirt' is a very English word," the *Duc* said. "I could express what I am attempting to do very much more eloquently in French. But if I am 'flirting' with you, why should you think it wrong?"

This was a direct question and Lina drew in her breath before she replied a little hesitatingly:

"You know . . . that I have a . . . husband."

"Who has taught you little or nothing about love."

Lina was silent, and after a moment he said:

"Husbands who do not look after their wives, especially if they are as beautiful as you, are of no consequence. While we are here alone under the stars, if we flirt as you call it, who would be hurt?"

"I would be, I would . . . know that I was . . . doing something . . . wrong," Lina said.

She could not help thinking as she spoke that it would, in fact, be very exciting to flirt with the *Duc*, to duel with him in words and listen to the things he wished to say to her.

But she thought if she did so, it would be not behaving in the way that Kitty expected.

She had promised that she was good, and surely

111

flirting with anybody, especially the *Duc*, was therefore something which was barred.

'Lady Birchington has been so kind to me,' Lina thought, 'bringing me here, giving me these expensive clothes. It would be very deceitful and dishonest to do anything behind her back of which she would not approve.'

"What is troubling you?" the *Duc* asked and his voice broke in on her thoughts.

"How do you...know I am...troubled?"

He smiled before he said:

"Your eyes are very revealing even in the starlight, and so are your lips."

It seemed to Lina as he spoke that he moved a little nearer to her and as she turned her face to look at him he said:

"At this moment I would give half my fortune to kiss you."

Lina's eyes met his and for a moment she was held spellbound. Then she put up her hands in an instinctive gesture of protest.

"Please...please, you are...frightening me!"

"In what way?" the *Duc* asked.

"I feel as if I am being...swept away on the waves of the sea...or perhaps by a...strong wind."

Her explanation was almost incoherent, and she thought there was a sudden light of triumph in the *Duc*'s eyes. She looked away from him again and said:

"Please...do not spoil this evening for me. I cannot explain...but it is so wonderful to be here...to see

Paris and the treasures in your house that it is . . . something I shall . . . remember all my . . . life."

"And it would spoil those memories if I made love to you?" the Duc asked.

"Y—yes."

"Why?"

"Because I have been . . . told that it is . . . something . . . I must not . . . listen to."

"I cannot understand," the Duc said. "Who has told you that you must not listen to me?"

Lina did not answer and he said:

"Has your husband extracted from you a vow of chastity before he allowed you to come to Paris? Or have you pledged yourself to somebody else?"

"I . . . I cannot answer your . . . questions," Lina said. "You make me . . . shy and embarrassed! I just want to think of how exciting it is to be here and be with somebody like you who could answer my questions . . . if you wished to do so."

"I cannot understand why you should feel like that," the *Duc* said, "but because I want you to be happy, Lina, I will do what you wish."

Because he had capitulated so unexpectedly and so quickly Lina turned towards him again with a smile.

"Thank y . . ." she began but when she met his eyes the words seemed to die on her lips.

She sat looking at him and although he did not move she felt as if he drew nearer and nearer and his eyes grew larger and larger until the whole world was filled with them and she could think of nothing else.

Only then, as they were motionless as if turned to stone, did they hear Kitty's laughter in the distance, and it broke the spell.

Lina awoke with an inescapable feeling that she had been dreaming of something which made her so happy she could feel it still in her mind and in her heart.

Then she was thinking of the *Duc* and the strange feelings he had aroused in her and knew she had gone to sleep thinking of him and that he had been with her all night in her dreams.

When Kitty had come back to where they were sitting she had insisted on taking Lina home saying they both needed their 'beauty sleep' before the Ball tomorrow night.

"We intend to shine dazzlingly in what we know, dear Fabian, will be a unique gathering of beautiful women, because they have all at one time or another been *admired* by you."

The way Kitty accentuated the word 'admire' made it quite obvious that she intended it to mean something much more emotional.

The *Duc* merely smiled and said lightly:

"I have never known a time, Kitty, when you have not shone almost blindingly!"

"Thank you," Kitty replied, "I shall be amused to see who receives your accolade as being the most beautiful guest present."

The *Duc* laughed.

"As I have no wish to be pierced by a thousand

daggers, I will be very careful to keep my choice to myself. A woman scorned can be far more dangerous on such occasions than any jealous man!"

"That is true," Kitty said. "And I am glad you are aware of it."

She looked at him meaningfully, Lina thought, and she wondered, although it seemed very unlikely, if Kitty was jealous because the *Duc* had stayed behind with her when she walked in the garden with the *Comte*.

Then she told herself that Kitty had brought her here especially to be with the *Duc*.

Nevertheless she could not help thinking that Kitty's attitude was a little strange, especially when as they drove back to where they were staying she said:

"What did the *Duc* say to you when you were alone?"

She spoke in a sharp voice that always made Lina feel uncomfortable, and she replied:

"We...talked on...several subjects."

"Did he make love to you?"

Again Kitty's voice was hard and because she felt she must tell the truth, Lina said:

"I think, because he is a Frenchman, he tried to flirt with me."

"Of course he did," Kitty snapped, "not because he is a Frenchman, but because he is himself, and he finds any new and pretty woman irresistible!"

"I...I would not...listen to him," Lina said quickly, "at least...I tried not to."

There was silence for a moment, and she thought

115

as Kitty said nothing she was pleased.

Then the horses came to a standstill outside where they were staying and Lina went upstairs, but Kitty who had been told that her hostess, the *Comtesse*, was in the Salon, went to join her.

Now with a thrill of delight because she was in Paris and it was another day, Lina sat up in bed.

As she did so she knew that she would see the *Duc* and also attend the Ball.

It was very exciting. At the same time she tried not to remember that she had thought of the *Duc* first and of the Ball second.

She dressed with the help of one of the house-maids with whom she conversed in French and asked her what part of France she came from, and then went downstairs.

Because it was still quite early she was sure Kitty would not have been called and she decided this was an opportunity for finding some books she could read.

She hoped one of them might describe the French families she would see this evening and of course that of the *Duc*.

There were a number of books exquisitely bound in an Ante-room which opened out of the Salon in which they had been sitting the day before, but when she entered she was first of all entranced by the pictures which were all by French artists.

She was standing looking at one when she heard somebody come into the room and turned to see her hostess, the *Comtesse* de la Tour.

She had not had a chance to speak to her since they

116

had arrived as the *Comtesse* appeared to be always out.

Now she realised that she was extremely *chic* as only a Frenchwoman could be. Although by no means beautiful, she was attractive in a way it was difficult to describe.

With dark hair and dark eyes which had a penetrating way of looking at whom she was speaking she was also, Lina thought, somewhat intimidating.

Her jewellery was fantastic, and the black pearls she wore round her neck and in her ears were something Lina had never seen before.

She looked at them and tried not to stare as she said:

"Bonjour, Madame! I was admiring your pictures. I have always longed to see a Boucher and this, I am sure, must be one of the best he ever painted!"

She spoke rather effusively because the way the *Comtesse* was looking at her made her feel uncomfortable and shy.

Then to her surprise the *Comtesse* closed the door behind her before she came further into the room.

"I wish to speak to you, Lady Littleton," she said in excellent English.

"But . . . of course," Lina replied.

The *Comtesse* was still staring at her, and now Lina felt as if she looked her up and down with what, although it seemed incredible, was an expression of hostility.

The *Comtesse* did not speak and after a moment Lina said nervously:

"H–have I done . . . anything to . . . upset you?"

117

"I understand," the *Comtesse* said speaking after a pause, "that you dined last night with the *Comte* du Pret and the *Duc* de Saverne."

"Yes," Lina replied. "Lady Birchington took me there."

"Lady Birchington took you!" the *Comtesse* said scornfully. "If you are honest, Lady Littleton, it was the *Duc* who proposed the dinner should take place."

"He certainly... mentioned it to... us when we were at his... house," Lina answered.

"I know his methods," the *Comtesse* said, "and I want to make something perfectly clear: the *Duc* belongs to me!"

Lina stared at the *Comtesse* in surprise and she went on:

"We are to be married in a very short while. It has been arranged for a long time, and I will not allow you or anybody else to interfere!"

"I have no... intention of... doing any such... thing!" Lina stammered.

"I know what you are doing," the *Comtesse* said. "I am not a fool and I can guess why Lady Birchington brought you to Paris. That woman has always hated me because I am and always have been part of Fabian's life."

The *Comtesse* paused for a moment, then made a gesture which made the rings on her fingers flash in the sunlight.

"But she is finished! Finished! He has no further use for her or those other stupid Englishwomen who tried to ensnare him. They are finished too!"

She spoke with such contempt and scorn in her voice that Lina could only listen in a mesmerised manner and feel it impossible to move or speak.

"Now he is mine!" the *Comtesse* went on, "and I will not have you interfering or trying to entice him into making love to you while he should be thinking of me."

"But I have...not done...that!" Lina protested, feeling she must somehow stop the *Comtesse* ranting at her in this intimidating manner.

"Do not lie to me!" the *Comtesse* stormed. "You are like all the rest of those love-starved English ladies whose husbands prefer sport to them."

"No...no! That is not...true where I am...concerned," Lina stammered.

"He will tire of you, make no mistake about that!" the *Comtesse* went on, as if she had not spoken, "just as he tired of Daisy Holme, Evie Pendock, Alice Whatever-her-name-was, and of course that red-headed friend of yours who hunted him like a tigress!"

The *Comtesse*'s voice broke and she snapped her fingers in the air before she said:

"I am rid of them all! They are finished—gone! And that is why I will not have you creeping in and trying to take him away from me. He is mine, mine, mine! Do you hear?"

The *Comtesse*'s words ended in a screech and it seemed to Lina that she looked distraught and so wild that instinctively she took a step backwards feeling almost as if she might attack her physically.

"You are...wrong, *Madame*," she said in a voice

that trembled, "and I promise you I have no . . . designs on the *Duc* none at all!"

"You need not lie because I do not believe you!" the *Comtesse* replied, "and I am warning you, as I shall warn Fabian, that I will no longer stand for such treatment. Make no mistake, I mean what I say!"

She stood for a moment shaking with rage. Then she turned and walked towards the door.

Only as she reached it did she look back to say:

"If I did what I wished to do, I would turn you out, here and now, and make sure you did not attend the Ball tonight. But it would only cause a scandal, so you can stay. But do not forget that I have warned you to leave Fabian alone."

She went out of the room as she finished speaking and slammed the door shut behind her.

Lina put her hands to her breast as if to soothe the wild beating of her heart.

Never had she thought that any woman would speak to her in such a manner and look so distraught as she did so.

The *Comtesse* was so frightening in her vehemence that now, even when she had gone, the room seemed to echo with the sound of her voice and the manner in which she had seemed almost to spit out her words.

If the *Duc* married her, as she clearly intended he should, Lina could not help feeling that she would make him unhappy.

Then she told herself it was none of her business: she would be wise after what had been said to keep out of the way of the *Duc* and make sure she did not incur the *Comtesse*'s wrath.

Then she remembered that Kitty and her friends expected something different.

Suddenly she remembered what the *Comtesse* had said, that they all three in the past had had flirtations with the *Duc* before he tired of them.

She might have suspected that, but now that it had been said openly it made her feel very uncomfortable.

"If they have had flirtations with him," she questioned to herself, "why should they have brought me to Paris, and why were they so insistent that I must be good and keep to the principles on which I have been brought up?"

Suddenly it came to her like a shaft of blinding light, and she understood.

As the *Comtesse* had said, they were all three of them part of the *Duc*'s past, and if she was to be believed he had become bored with them before they were bored with him.

Now, Lina thought, she understood so many things which had eluded her before.

The reason she was here was that Daisy, Evie, and Kitty hoped that the *Duc* would fall in love with her and she would refuse to listen to him.

It seemed almost a childish game. But how could they have been so sure that he would try to flirt with her as, in fact, he had done last night?

It was also perplexing that they had insisted on her having a husband.

121

Surely it would have been much more simple if she had come as herself, a young girl in whom it would not have been in the least reprehensible if he had tried to flirt with her, and she could have listened to him without being disloyal or... unfaithful.

Then as that last word came to her mind Lina was suddenly very still.

It was impossible! She could not believe it! And yet insidiously as if a serpent hissed the truth into her mind she knew that the *Duc* had tempted Kitty, Daisy, and Evie into being unfaithful to their husbands!

She could not believe such reprehensible behaviour was possible where any Lady was concerned. And yet, as if the pieces of the puzzle at last fell into place, she understood what in her ignorance had seemed so incomprehensible before.

"How could they?" she asked herself, and felt it was the most shocking and horrifying thing that could possibly happen.

Then vaguely she remembered people talking about the behaviour of the Prince of Wales.

They had laughed at his infatuations for Lily Langtry, then for Lady Brooke, and now his *close friendship* accentuating the word, with Mrs. Keppel, and now she supposed it was the same relationship the *Duc* had had with The Three Beauties.

Lina felt as if the room was swinging round her. She groped for a chair, sat down on it, and tried to reason things out for herself.

She had not the slightest idea what a man and woman did when they made love. She only knew that if they were not married it was a sin which was condemned by the Church.

Because it had never entered her world until now she had not thought about people making love, except that it was something wonderful which had happened to her father and mother.

They had fallen in love with each other the moment they met, and had been supremely happy together, despite the fact that they had so little money.

She also knew that she had been born because they were married, and because children were the result of people being in love.

But now she thought of it, there had been a child in the village who was spoken of with scorn and in lowered voices because it had no father.

Lina had always meant to ask her mother to explain this to her, but somehow she had forgotten, and after her mother was dead there was no-one else with whom to discuss such things.

'I do not understand,' she thought now and decided once again that she must be mistaken.

She could however, see in her mind's eye Kitty looking up at the *Duc* with an expression in her green eyes that had not been there when she spoke to anybody else.

She remembered too while they planned the journey to Paris, the way in which Daisy's voice would soften when she spoke the *Duc*'s name and Evie's would somehow sound caressing when she was not being spiteful.

"I will not believe it! I will not!" Lina said aloud,

but while her voice said one thing, her brain said another.

"How could he? And so many of them!" she asked herself.

There had been others also, women with whom he had become bored after a few months.

"It is horrid, and I do not want to think about it," Lina said aloud.

She jumped up from the chair to go to the bookcase to look for something to read which might take her thoughts away from the *Duc* then she remembered that she had been looking for a history of his ancestors.

"I do not want to know anything more about him," she said.

The day passed slowly because Kitty was determined to rest before the Ball.

She therefore made no effort to do anything but lie looking extremely beautiful on a sofa with her feet up and talk to Daisy and Evie when they came to luncheon.

There was no sign of the *Comtesse* and when one of them mentioned her, Kitty said:

"Yvonne told me she was going over to Fabian's house to help him with the plans for this evening. Every guest has been allotted to a dinner-party which I imagine is quite a Herculean task on its own."

"Yvonne will enjoy that," Daisy replied. "She likes to think of herself as Fabian's right-hand, or something even more intimate."

"She will doubtless get him in the end," Evie said. "Those persistent women are like leeches and one cannot shake them off."

The bitter way she spoke revealed only too clearly, Lina thought unhappily, that her supposition concerning the part Evie had played in the *Duc*'s life was true.

She suddenly wanted to say she had no wish to go to the Ball after all!

But she could imagine the astonishment there would be on the beautiful faces of the women sitting round the table, and the manner in which she would be cross-questioned as to why she wished to go back to England.

It would be impossible to tell them the truth, Lina thought, and there was nothing she could do.

Yet she felt she could not face the *Duc* again or listen to his deep voice saying things which evoked a very strange response within herself that she did not wish to think about.

Both Daisy and Evie had been extremely curious as to what had happened the night before.

"What did the *Duc* say to you when you were alone with him, Lina?" Daisy asked.

Lina felt that both she and Evie spoke to her in the same way, as if they were questioning a servant or a young Governess.

She suddenly resented their manner and the assumption that she must reply to their questions because she was under an obligation to them.

"Lina said she thought the *Duc* was trying to flirt with her," Kitty said.

"Of course!" Evie answered. "Was he likely to do anything else?"

"What did you say to him?" Daisy asked.

Again because she did not reply Kitty interposed:

"She refused to listen to him. That must have been a surprise!"

"I want to know what he said, word for word," Daisy insisted.

There was silence until Lina said:

"I am sorry... but I am... afraid I have... forgotten. It all happened very... quickly. Lady Birchington was not... away for... long."

Daisy looked at Kitty accusingly.

"That was stupid of you, Kitty!" she said. "You know as well as I do that Fabian likes to work up to a dramatic situation smoothly, like music rising rhythmically in a crescendo."

She gave a little laugh.

"That is rather apt, is it not? But you know what I am trying to say."

"I think I was away quite long enough," Kitty said defensively. "After all, it would be a great mistake to have her boring him too soon."

They were talking of Lina as if she was of so little importance that she might not have been there.

She wanted to say that the whole thing was wrong from the very start, and she wished to play no further part in this foolish charade.

But even as she thought it, she knew that she could not bring herself to sacrifice her chance of attending the Ball.

It was the only Ball she might ever go to, a Ball she would have to remember for the rest of her life.

"What is the use of having principles, if one cannot afford them?" she asked and knew that for the first time in her life she was being cynical.

It was an inexpressible relief when Daisy and Evie left to go back to where they were staying and as they were saying goodbye Daisy remarked:

"You never told us what Yvonne thinks of Lina."

Kitty laughed.

"She has not said anything to me, but she looked at her in a way that was far more expressive than words!"

They all laughed, but it seemed rather contrived laughter which Lina thought was somehow superficial.

Because in a way she was still suffering from the shock of the *Comtesse*'s attack on her and of recognising the truth which lay behind the facade, she was delighted when she and Kitty were alone.

"I am going to lie down," Kitty said, "and I suggest you do the same. I think actually you are looking rather pale, but you must look your best tonight, for the competition will, I assure you, be very fierce."

She laughed before she added:

"In fact it will be a miracle if the *Duc* asks you for even one dance. But we must just hope!"

Lina wanted to reply that she had no wish to dance with the *Duc* then she knew that would not be true.

She would like to dance with him just because it would be another memory to add to her scrapbook.

Then she found herself wondering what he would say to her, and if everything he said was a repetition of what he had said before to Daisy, Evie, Kitty, Alice and perhaps dozens of other women.

"He is despicable," she told herself as she lay on her bed with the blinds half-drawn.

And yet, instead of hating him, as she told herself

she should do, she could not help when she shut her eyes, seeing his face.

Different as it was from any man's face she had ever seen before, she had known from the very first, he was exactly as she had expected him to be.

He was a rake and a roué, a man no sensible woman would trust. And yet he was also unique, original and however much he might not deserve it, he was what the English called a 'gentleman'.

'If I were a writer, I would write a book about him,' Lina thought, 'but the difficulty would be whether he should be the hero or the villain.'

Then it struck her that perhaps all men were a little of both, but where the *Duc* was concerned, because he was such a vital person, the two parts of his nature were both overwhelming instead of being average and normal as other men's were.

Once again she could hear his voice and knew that wrong or right, good or bad, when he said the word 'love' it did something very strange to her heart.

When the housemaid came to prepare Lina's bath she brought into the room a cardboard box tied with silver ribbon and a note.

"For you, *Madame*," she said. "It came sometime ago, but as I thought you were asleep I did not like to disturb you."

"For me?" Lina asked.

She sat up in bed to take the box and look at the note.

There was no need to wonder from whom it had come, one look at the strong, upright writing told Lina who had written her name, and she sat staring at the envelope as if she was afraid to open it.

Then slowly she did so, and pulled out the sheet of paper inside.

There was no need to look at the address embossed on top of the paper, or the *Duc's* coronet above it. Her eyes rested on only two lines of writing:

"Until tonight when we will exchange ideas and read each other's thoughts."

Lina stared at it.

It was not the sort of message she would have expected him to send her.

Yet, because it was unexpected and not in the least fulsome, it somehow seemed to calm down her feelings against him and make his behaviour seem less outrageous then it had when she came upstairs to lie down.

Quickly, because she did not want to think too deeply about him, she opened the box.

She expected flowers, and she was not expecting that inside there was first sheet upon sheet of tissue paper, then in the centre of it a small case of deep blue velvet.

She opened it and saw to her astonishment a diamond star.

It was exquisite, at the same time something which must have cost a great deal of money and Lina stared at it incredulously.

How could he think, how could he imagine for one second, that she would accept such a valuable present from any man whom she had just met? All the more so because she was supposed to be a married woman.

Then she found herself wondering if he had given such presents to Kitty, Daisy, and Evie, and if so, had they returned them?

Because it was a question she could not answer, it suddenly struck Lina that perhaps if she told Kitty what she had received from the *Duc* she would be forced to keep it.

And that, she knew, was something she would never do in any circumstances.

Her mother had told her that a lady should never accept presents from a gentleman unless they were engaged to be married.

"Chocolates, scent, and sometimes gloves are permissible," her mother had said, "but never, never jewellery, except as an engagement present."

She had laughed as she spoke, adding:

"It is unlikely that anybody will offer you jewellery, but sometimes the unexpected happens, and it is always wise to know beforehand what is right and what is wrong."

Lina had hardly listened at the time, but now she knew the unexpected had happened. She had received a present which must be returned.

The difficulty was how to do so.

Quickly she got out of bed and while the housemaid was away collecting cans of water for her bath she hid the velvet box at the back of one of her drawers.

Then she picked one of the flowers out of a vase

of roses which stood on a table in the window and put it inside the cardboard box.

She was quite certain that the maid would be curious about what she had received, and would doubtless tell Smith who would tell Kitty.

If she said the *Duc* had sent her a rose it might seem to mean something special. She could easily say that as it did not go with her gown she could not wear it.

She put the lid on the box and laid it casually on the dressing-table.

Then as she was dressing she tried to think of how she could convey to the *Duc* that his present was not only unwelcome but in fact insulting.

The *Comtesse* was giving a large dinner-party before the Ball and as the guests arrived, each woman seeming to Lina to be more beautiful and more exquisitely gowned than the last, she could not help wondering how many of them had meant something to the *Duc*?

How many of them had received presents like the one she had hidden upstairs?

Even though it seemed incredible, she was more suspicious of the emeralds Kitty was wearing round her neck, the diamonds and sapphires that made Daisy glitter like a Christmas Tree, and the turquoises and pearls which were extremely becoming to Evie.

Then she told herself she was being utterly ridiculous.

All three of The Beauties had husbands, and she was quite certain that because they were gentlemen

131

like her father they would never contemplate allowing their wives to wear jewels given them by another man.

If that was so, why had the *Duc* sent her a present that would make any jealous husband challenge him to a duel?

"I do not understand," she told herself and thought that this was yet another of the incomprehensible problems for which she had to find an answer.

When dinner was over and the ladies went upstairs to get their wraps before proceeding to the Ball Lina resisted an impulse to have another look at the diamond star which lay hidden in her drawer.

It might be a reprehensible present, but at least it was a beautiful one.

Then she told herself that when she got the chance she would make it very clear to the Duc that she was extremely surprised by his present and that she would return it to him tomorrow.

Whatever effect he had on her, she must remember that every word he said was a mere repetition of what he had said to all the other women who had been foolish enough to listen to him.

'He is the type of man against whom young girls should be warned,' she thought.

Then she remembered that the *Duc* did not think of her as a young girl, but as a married woman, and if he was behaving badly, so indeed was she.

She was deceiving him, acting a lie, and was his guest entirely under false pretences.

'I suppose actually we are two of a kind,' she thought irrepressibly.

She felt she could almost see his eyes twinkling and the twist of his lips as they mocked at her.

"'People in glasshouses...'" she murmured.

But she was smiling as she went down the stairs to join the dinner-party guests who were in a hurry to get to the Ball.

Chapter Six

LINA LOOKED around her with delight.

She could not imagine anything could be more exciting and romantic than the scene the *Duc* had created in his Ball-Room and garden.

When she had seen it the previous day it had seemed to her very lovely and exciting because it represented Venice, a place she had always longed to visit.

But now the painted fantasy seemed to have become the reality of dreams which carried her away to become part of the music and the stars overhead.

At this, her first Ball, she thought as she watched the dancers that nothing could be more graceful or more elegant than the ladies with their glittering jewels and full-skirted gowns being swung round by the gentlemen in their white shirts and tail-coats.

"I must remember every moment of it!" Lina told herself.

But from the moment she arrived she found it hard to look at anybody except the *Duc*.

Even amongst the crowd of his guests he stood out

and whomever she was dancing with, Lina found her eyes being irresistibly drawn to his face and she found herself listening for the sound of his voice.

He was dancing, she saw, first with the older women who were, although she was unable to name them, obviously those belonging to the ancient families of France.

They had an aristocratic air about them and a pride which Lina felt came from years and generations of authority. It made them hold their heads high and move as if even when dancing they condescended to those of less importance than themselves.

The band in the Ball-Room was as the *Duc* had promised, composed mainly of violins, but outside in the garden there were wandering musicians playing guitars and singing Italian love-songs.

These blended in with the lights swinging on the ends of the Gondolas and the cries of the boatmen as they warned other craft to keep out of their way.

It was all so thrilling that Lina stood on the terrace looking at it wide-eyed and she started when a voice beside her asked:

"Are you enjoying yourself, Lady Littleton?"

She turned to see an elderly woman wearing a magnificent tiara whose throat was draped in pearls and to whom she had been presented on arrival.

Lina knew she was the *Duchesse* de Saverne and the *Duc*'s grandmother.

"It is wonderful, *Madame*!" Lina replied. "I could not imagine anything could look so lovely!"

"I am glad you appreciate it," the *Duchesse* said.

"But so much money could have been spent on a better cause."

It was almost what Lina had said herself to be snubbed by Kitty for having such Socialistic ideas.

"I wish instead," the *Duchesse* went on, "that my grandson's friends from England could have come here to celebrate his wedding."

"The *Duc* is to be married?" Lina asked thinking that was what the *Duchesse* was telling her.

The old lady shook her head.

"Unfortunately no, but you will understand, Lady Littleton, that we of his family who love him want him to settle down and choose a wife."

The way she spoke and the sharp glance of her eyes made Lina uncomfortably aware that the *Duchesse* had a very good reason for speaking to her in such a way.

She was quite sure that somebody had told the *Duc*'s grandmother that he had a new interest and she was therefore being warned that she was an intruder and his family were not pleased at his choice.

The *Duchesse* was obviously waiting for her to speak and after a moment Lina said:

"I feel . . . sure the *Duc* will . . . eventually do what is . . . right for his . . . family and for the . . . position he . . . occupies."

"What is right," the *Duchesse* said, "is that he should marry somebody whose family is the equal of his own. As you are doubtless aware, Lady Littleton, in France most marriages are arranged simply because it would be unthinkable for somebody in my grandson's position to make a *misalliance*."

137

She paused and as Lina did not speak she went on:

"That noble blood should join with noble blood is something that is ingrained into the conscience of every French aristocrat from the time he is born. Tradition means a great deal to us here in France."

Lina understood now exactly what the *Duchesse* was saying to her.

She might have a title, she might outwardly appear the equal of the *Duc*, but his relations wanted him to marry and not indulge in *affaires de coeur* with women whom they did not consider important enough from a social point of view.

Lina wanted to ask if she thought the same about Daisy, Evie, and Kitty and she wondered if the Dowager would be honest enough to say 'Yes'.

She knew how proud the French were, especially those who belonged to the *ancien régime* who had never really accepted the titles created by Napoleon Bonaparte.

It made her smile to think that in naming her for the role she had to play in enticing the *Duc*, Daisy, Kitty, and Evie had not aimed high enough.

'They should have made me a Duchess!' Lina thought.

But she knew that title would have been too easy to check if it had been a false one.

Finding this conversation with the *Duc*'s grandmother most uncomfortable, she was relieved when her partner in the last dance came hurrying back to her with a glass of champagne in his hand.

"I lost you, *Madame*," he said, "and I have been

so long because unfortunately there was no lemonade to be found. I hope instead champagne will quench your thirst."

"Thank you," Lina said. "It is very kind of you."

She took a small sip from the glass and as she did so realised that the *Duchesse* had moved away.

"Will you dance with me again?" the Frenchman asked. "There is no need for me to tell you that I have no wish to dance with anybody but you, and if you refuse my whole evening will be ruined!"

He was speaking in French which made his words seem more insistent and more ardent than they would have sounded in English, and Lina laughed as she replied:

"You are very flattering, *Monsieur*, but I am already engaged for the next three dances."

"Then you must give me the fourth," the Frenchman said, and took her programme from her to write his name in it.

But somehow as the evening progressed Lina found it impossible to keep strictly to her promises.

The Ball had started formally and because it was in the *Duc*'s house everybody was behaving correctly and without undue exuberance.

But the romantic atmosphere of the setting and perhaps also the excellent champagne which was being carried round by footmen wearing powdered wigs, made the tempo rise as the music of the violins seemed to rise with it.

There was excitement in the air and everything, Lina thought, seemed to sparkle and shimmer until it became part of herself and she sparkled too.

As she replied to the compliments which she was paid and the flattery of her partners she thought that she was unusually witty, and now she felt not that she was listening to the dialogue of a play, but was taking part in it.

Every man with whom she danced begged her to go with him in a Gondola on the water, but having watched the Gondolas gliding away into the shadows under the 'Bridge of Sighs', Lina felt this would be indiscreet.

She was quite certain that if she went with any man, whoever he might be, alone in a Gondola, he would make love to her and if nothing else would insist upon holding her hand.

She had no wish for this to happen and most of all she had no desire for any man to touch her—except, to be honest, one.

She was embarrassed by the thought, and yet she felt as the evening wore on and the *Duc* did not approach her, that she was waiting, longing, and yearning and in a way she could not explain sending out vibrations to call him to her.

"I want to talk to him...I want to dance with him," she whispered when it was getting late and they had not spoken since her arrival.

She could not understand why he was avoiding her. She saw him dancing with Kitty, then with Daisy, and she supposed Evie would be the next.

She became aware suddenly that the glittering scene

did not seem quite as lovely as it had been, and there was a little lump of disappointment within her breast heavy as a stone.

Then as the music started again and she moved away from her partner with whom she had been talking on the terrace to go back into the Ball-Room suddenly the *Duc* was beside her.

He did not speak, but merely put his arm around her and drew her onto the polished floor. She found they were dancing to a dreamy Waltz, and she felt as if she had stepped once again into a dream.

Every one of her partners had told her how perfectly she danced and how light she was in their arms.

With the *Duc* she felt as if she melted into him and they were not two people dancing together, but one.

At the same time she was vividly conscious of his hand on her waist, his arm enfolding her, his other hand holding hers.

When she looked up at him she thought for some reason she could not understand that he looked serious and even a little grim.

"I have been...waiting," she said, "to tell you how...wonderful this...evening is."

"Is it really wonderful for you?" he asked and there was a deep note in his voice.

"Very...very...wonderful!" Lina replied.

"I think when I chose this background for my Ball I must have known that you would be here, and there is no need for me to tell you that there is no one else in the room as beautiful as you!"

The way he spoke, very quietly in a voice that seemed to throb with sincerity, made Lina's heart turn over in her breast.

She looked up at him and saw there was not the mocking smile on his lips that she expected, nor did his eyes seem to be twinkling as they had before.

Instead he looked at her just for one brief moment, then he pulled her a little closer to him and they moved around the room without speaking.

Before the dance came to an end the *Duc* stopped at one of the windows leading out onto the terrace and drew Lina through it and out into the garden.

They walked down some steps and when they were level with the lake there was a Gondola waiting and he helped her into it.

They sat side by side on the red silk cushions with the boatman behind them and as the Gondola moved slowly with its lights reflected golden on the water Lina looked up at the *Duc*.

She saw he was looking ahead in the direction they were travelling.

He did not speak, and as she knew perceptively that he had a reason for not doing so she was silent too.

She was also aware that anything they said could be overheard by the boatman behind them.

Although she could see other couples on the water clasped in each other's arms or talking with their lips very close she was aware she had no wish for anything she and the *Duc* said to each other to be overheard.

As the Gondola carried them away from the house and the music from the Band receded into the distance, it was easier to hear the wandering musicians playing the passionate, throbbing love-songs that seemed to accelerate the beat of the heart.

It made Lina feel that it was hard to breathe, there was a little constriction in her throat, and she was so acutely conscious of the *Duc* that although there was a space between them on the cushioned seat she felt almost as if she was in his arms.

The Gondola passed under the 'Bridge of Sighs,' then there were fewer lanterns and the artificial lake curved away into a wilder part of the garden which was filled with shrubs and trees.

At the far end of the lake there was a landing place and without any orders the Gondolier stopped.

Lina looked at the *Duc* enquiringly and as she stepped out he held out his hand to assist her also to alight.

She felt herself quiver at the touch of his fingers.

Without even thinking of what she was doing she had, while they were travelling in the Gondola, pulled off her long kid gloves and now her arms were bare.

They walked up a flight of steps and in front of them there was what to Lina looked like a screen of leaves which the *Duc* pulled to one side.

For a moment because she was surprised she hesitated and looked back to see the Gondola which had brought them there moving away towards the distant lights.

"He will return when we are ready," the *Duc* said quietly as if he would reassure her.

They were the first words he had spoken since they

had left the Ball-Room. Lina smiled at him and went through the curtain of leaves he was holding to one side.

Then she gave a little gasp, for inside she saw there was arranged what was obviously a 'sitting-out' place for the dancers but so beautiful and so unusual that she could only stare in amazement.

The walls of the arbour, if that was what it was, were made entirely of flowers, fixed to trellis-work, and so skillfully done that it became a bower of blossom.

It was all lighted from behind so that the flowers were transparent against the light—roses, carnations, lilies, orchids, every imaginable sort of flower!

The scent of them filled the air and mingled with the music, which was now so far away that it was difficult to know if one really heard it, or if it merely lingered like a melody in one's memory.

There was a large comfortable couch covered with silk cushions, and like the floor it was sprinkled with the petals from the flowers which made the whole place seem fairy-like.

"It is lovely!" Lina breathed. "I could not imagine anything could be so lovely or so unusual."

"That is what I wanted you to think," the *Duc* said, "because I designed this place especially so that I could bring you here and talk to you."

Lina gave him a little nervous glance from under her eye-lashes, before she said:

"I also want to ... talk to you ... about the present you ... sent me."

"I hoped you would wear it," the *Duc* replied.

She shook her head.

"I cannot do that...and please...I do not want to...hurt your feelings...but it is something I... cannot...accept."

"Why not?"

"Because it would be wrong to take...anything so...valuable from...somebody who has no...right to give it to...me."

She thought as she spoke that she sounded a little incoherent, but it was difficult to put into words, and she was also afraid the *Duc* would think her ungrateful and rude in refusing his gift.

He did not speak and because she was nervous she clasped her hands together and said:

"Please...try to...understand. I have been... brought up to think it is wrong for a...lady to accept any...present from a man which is not something trivial...like flowers...and I know that... Mama would not...approve if I kept your star...beautiful though it is."

"You say your mother would not approve," the *Duc* said, "but surely it should be your husband's attitude which should concern you?"

"Y—yes...of course," Lina said quickly, "and he would not...approve...either."

"I had a reason for giving you that particular present," the *Duc* said, "which I will explain. But first, Lina, I want to look at you which I have been afraid to do until now."

"Afraid?"

"Do you suppose that if I had looked at you I would have been able to go on dancing with other women, talking to them, playing host?"

His voice deepened as he said:

"I have been counting the minutes until I could dance with you, until I could bring you here and tell you that I love you!"

Lina gave a little gasp and put her hands up to her breast.

"N–no . . . please . . ."

"Please—what?" the *Duc* asked. "You know as well as I do that we mean something to each other that cannot be put into words."

He put his arms out towards her as he spoke and Lina gave a little cry and moved away from him.

The arbour was very small, and she could only move a few steps before she stood with her back against the wall of flowers.

"I . . . I think I should . . . go back . . . I must not stay here . . . alone with you."

"But you want to," the *Duc* said. "Tell me the truth, Lina. You want to stay. You want to hear what I have to say."

She knew that was the truth, and for a moment it was impossible to lie, impossible to play the part that was expected of her.

She knew the *Duc* was looking at her and that if she met his eyes she would do anything he wanted.

"Please . . . let me . . . go!"

She spoke almost as if he was holding her.

"I cannot do that for the moment," the *Duc* answered.

"Why . . . not?"

"Because you have to listen to what I have to say," he said, "and perhaps I should do things in the right order."

There was something in the way he spoke that sounded strange and Lina said:

"I . . . do not . . . understand."

"Why should you?" he asked. "And yet I think deep down inside you, because we think the same and are the same, you will understand."

Lina was silent and the *Duc* said:

"I sent you that present tonight for a very special reason, because it symbolises what you are to me."

"A . . . star?" Lina whispered beneath her breath.

"Exactly!" the *Duc* said. "And stars, as you know, my lovely one, are out of reach."

There was a strange note in his voice as he spoke the last words and he went on:

"That is what you are to me, a star in the sky above me, perfect in its beauty, entrancing, beguiling, but I cannot touch it, and I cannot make it mine."

The way he spoke seemed to vibrate in Lina's heart, and she felt herself quiver, but she did not interrupt and the *Duc* continued:

"When I built this bower of flowers I was thinking of you. I meant to bring you here tonight to make love to you, and convince you that we belong to each other, and there is nothing else of any importance in the world for you or for me except love."

Because of the way he spoke Lina trembled and her fingers were clasped together so tightly that it was painful.

147

"I was sure I would be able to persuade you," the *Duc* went on, "as I have persuaded other women before. But I suddenly knew that you were different."

"D—different?"

"Different from all the other women to whom I have made love and who have been part of my life for a short time."

The *Duc* made an impatient movement as he said:

"There is no need to confess to you that my reputation is well-deserved, but let me say in self-defence, I have never taken a woman who was unwilling or forced myself upon her."

It flashed through Lina's mind that no woman to whom the *Duc* made love would ever be unwilling.

"This afternoon," he said, "when I went to buy you a present which would have been one of gratitude to thank you for a love which I was sure you would give me, I saw the diamond star."

The *Duc* paused for a moment before he said, and his voice was very deep and moving:

"Then I knew that was what you were, and I could not spoil anything that was so perfect."

Lina drew in her breath.

"Yes—perfect!" he went on. "Perfect in a way no other woman has ever been and as no other woman has ever touched my heart."

He made a sound that was half a groan and half a sigh as he added:

"I cannot spoil you or make you unhappy as I have made other women. I never meant to hurt them, but I often did. That is something which must never happen to you, and if I made you cry I think I would want to kill myself!"

"Are you...really saying this to...me?" Lina asked.

"You must try to understand, my precious one," the *Duc* answered, "that what I feel for you is real love—love so overwhelming, so different from anything I have ever felt before, that I can only recognise it as a gift from God."

He reached forward and very gently took Lina's hand in his as he said:

"That is why, my precious little star, we are going to say goodbye to each other tonight and I shall never see you again."

"Oh...no...!" Lina cried. "I cannot...bear it!"

"It is something which has to happen," the *Duc* said, "because you have a husband, and because I am going to send you back to England perfect and unspoiled by the love of a man who can never mean anything serious in your life and could only disrupt and perhaps destroy you."

The way the *Duc* spoke was so sad and so touching that Lina felt the tears coming into her eyes.

It flashed through her mind that she could tell him the truth, but she knew that if she did so it would not make things any better.

In the first place she would be behaving disloyally and dishonourably to Kitty who had brought her here and spent a great deal of money in doing so. And, what was more, if the *Duc* knew she was unmarried, from his point of view it would make things even worse than they were already.

If he would not spoil her life as a married woman, he would certainly not feel differently about one who was unmarried.

Because she could think of nothing to say Lina only asked almost childishly:

"How . . . will it be . . . possible not to see you . . . again before I leave . . . Paris?"

"You will not see me," the *Duc* answered, "because I am going away. It will be very difficult for me to leave you behind, but it is something that must be done. Otherwise, my lovely Star, I may weaken in my resolution to do what is right."

He looked down at her as if he was imprinting the image of her face on his memory before he said:

"I shall think about you, dream about you, and you will be in my heart for ever!"

"How . . . can you . . . say that?" Lina asked.

"I say it because it is the truth," the *Duc* replied. "There are no words to explain the vibrations which pass between us. There is no need for words to explain that you belong to me and I belong to you, or that our spirits are closer than if our bodies were touching."

He drew in a deep breath before he said:

"*Le Bon Dieu* knows that the temptations of St. Anthony are nothing to what I am experiencing now."

His fingers tightened on her as he said:

"I want you, Lina! I want you unbearably, and because, my darling, you are already an indivisible part of me, I know that it would be impossible for you to resist me if I was determined to make you mine."

The passion in his voice and the sudden fire in his eyes made Lina quiver and as he felt her fingers move beneath his the *Duc* said:

"I know you were meant for me, and I know, whatever your marriage has been like, you are still essentially pure and innocent and have no conception of what real love can mean between a man and a woman when physically they are united by an uncontrollable flame of desire."

He hesitated before he added:

"That is what I feel with you. We would burn together in an ecstasy that would carry us on invisible wings into a Heaven of our own."

Lina gave an inarticulate little murmur and he said:

"You respond to me when I am talking to you, my lovely one, and if I were touching you it would be an indescribable rapture."

As the Duc spoke Lina could feel the rapture he spoke of moving within her.

It was like a little flame flickering through her body, then it became more insistent and she felt as if her whole being reached out towards him and she longed with an intensity that was painful to be close in his arms.

"I love you!" the Duc said. "I love you until I can see nobody else and hear nobody else. The whole world and the sky seem to be filled with you, and you alone."

"I love . . . you!" Lina breathed.

The words were only a whisper but the *Duc* heard them, and now she raised her face to his and looked up into his eyes.

Just as last night when they had looked at each other, she felt that she gave herself to him and he reached out towards her and they were no longer two people, but one.

For a long, long moment they stood looking at each other.

Then to Lina there were only the *Duc*'s dark eyes and him in the whole world.

Slowly, very slowly, he put his arms round her.

She felt as he did so as if he was lifting her into a special Heaven which belonged only to them. She was no longer afraid or alone, but his love filled her mind, her heart, and her body.

"I . . . love . . . you!"

Although the words were just the breath of a sigh, she felt as if she shouted them from the top of a mountain.

"This is goodbye, my precious one," the *Duc* said hoarsely.

Then his lips were on hers.

His kiss was all the rapture and the wonder which Lina had expected, but so much more.

Every word he had said about their love being an ecstasy and carrying them into a Heaven of their own was true.

As his arms drew her closer and still closer and his lips became more insistent, passionate, and possessive, she knew that the *Duc* was right in saying they were meant for each other.

She also believed him when he said what he felt for her was different from what he had ever felt for any other woman.

This was the love of two people who had met each other across eternity, this was the love about which there could be no pretence, no reservations.

It was a love that was perfect, divine, and everything that was false and untrue was purified by the fire of it.

As the *Duc* kissed her and went on kissing her Lina felt she had never lived until this moment and in kissing her he gave her life itself.

She was no longer human, no longer even herself, she was part, as he was, of the spirit of love and through them both poured the very essence of the Divine and for the moment they were gods....

Slowly, very slowly, the *Duc* raised his head and although he did not speak Lina knew this was the end.

Her heart was beating frantically, her whole being was infused with a rapture and a radiance which made her feel she was floating in an indefinable space enveloped in a celestial light.

Yet although he said nothing, she was aware that he was already retreating from her, leaving her and almost before she had become aware of it he would be gone, and she would be alone for the rest of her life.

She wanted to cry out at the cruelty of it, she wanted to hold onto him to prevent him from going but already she was standing by herself and his arms were no longer around her.

She knew that now they would travel back to the house the way they had come in a Gondola in silence, but apart.

Because it was an indescribable agony to find a love she had never known before and to realise that she must lose it tremblingly she put out her hand.

Even as she did so the curtain of leaves over the entrance parted and somebody came into the arbour.

For a moment Lina could not come back to reality and focus her eyes. Then she saw that it was a woman—the *Comtesse*.

"Just as I expected!" she said and her voice sounded crude and ugly against the background of the flowers and the distant music. "I thought I would find you here!"

"What do you want, Yvonne?" the *Duc* enquired.

"What do you expect me to want?" the *Comtesse* replied. "You, of course! As I have wanted you for years!"

"This is not the place for a scene . . ." the *Duc* began.

"A scene?" the *Comtesse* interrupted him. "Is that what you call it? *Alors*, I have had enough, Fabian, enough of your philandering, enough of your women! I came here tonight intending to kill this latest creature you are seducing, but I have changed my mind, and instead I intend to kill you!"

As she spoke the *Comtesse* brought up her hand from the folds of her evening gown and Lina saw that she held a small revolver in her hand.

"Now, Yvonne, be sensible!" the *Duc* said quietly. "It is not the moment to behave in an hysterical manner."

The *Comtesse* merely pointed the revolver at him as she said:

"What you call 'hysterical' is love, Fabian! And when you die, I shall suffer no longer."

As she spoke Lina realised from the expression in her eyes and the twist of her lips that the *Comtesse* was mad.

She had thought that she was deranged when she had ranted at her this morning, and now she knew unmistakably that the Frenchwoman was insane and that if she said she intended to kill she would do so.

Without thinking, without pausing for even a second, Lina threw herself in front of the *Duc* as the *Comtesse*'s voice rising to a strange, unearthly shriek cried:

"Die, Fabian! Die! And I hope you enjoy the kiss of death!"

As she spoke she pulled the trigger and there was an explosion which seemed to Lina to break her eardrums.

Then there was a burning, fiery agony which made her scream before darkness came down from overhead and covered her.

Chapter Seven

LINA CAME slowly back to consciousness from what seemed an endless dark tunnel.

For a long time she could not think of anything except that she was breathing, and it was strange to be doing so because something horrible had happened.

Then she slipped away again into the darkness, still uncertain of her thoughts and herself. . . .

───────────── • ─────────────

When she was conscious again she was aware there were birds singing. Somebody was moving and she could hear the swish of their clothes which was somehow different from sounds she had heard before.

Slowly, almost as if it might hurt, she opened her eyes.

She was in a room she did not know. It was dim, not because as she had first thought it was night, but because there were blinds over the windows to shut out the sun.

Then somebody leaned over her and gently lifting

her head held a drink to her lips. At the same time she was aware that she was thirsty and her mouth was dry.

"*Dormez, ma Petite!*" a kind voice said.

Because it seemed almost like a command she shut her eyes and slipped away into a dream again.

———————————————

A long time later, it might have been days or weeks, her brain felt clear and she knew she could think and feel. It was then she knew that something was constraining her left arm and when she tried to move it she gave a little murmur of pain.

Instantly somebody was at her bedside and she heard the voice she had heard before when she had been semi-conscious say in French:

"Are you awake, *Madame*?"

She looked up and saw a kind, serene face which was framed in a wimple and veil.

As if she had asked the question which would somehow not come to her lips, the Nun said:

"It is all right. You are better and there is no need to be afraid."

"A–afraid?" Lina questioned in her mind, thinking it was a strange word.

Then she remembered!

It flashed through her mind almost as if she saw a picture of what had taken place in front of her: the *Comtesse* holding a revolver, the mad note in her voice as she cried:

"Die, Fabian, die! And I hope you enjoy the kiss of death!"

Then Lina could hear the explosion and feel the sudden agony which had followed it.

"She . . . she shot . . . me!" she murmured in a whisper.

"Yes, you were shot," the Nun said quietly, "but by the blessing of God it did far less damage than might have been expected."

Slowly Lina turned her head and tried to look at her left shoulder.

Now she could see it above the bed-clothes and realised it was swathed in bandages.

"I have not . . . lost my . . . arm?" she asked in a frightened voice.

The Nun smiled.

"No, of course not. It was actually just a flesh wound, but the bullet had to be extracted and that means it will take a little time to heal. But you are young and strong, and we are praying for you."

"Thank . . . you," Lina said.

The Nun moved from the bedside to fetch a glass which contained a drink which tasted of fruit and honey.

She lifted Lina's head. Then she said:

"Would you like to sit up a little higher, *Madame*?"

"Yes . . . please," Lina said.

Very carefully the Nun lifted her and placed another pillow behind her head.

Then she went to the window and drew up the sun-blind a little so that more light came into the room.

Lina looked around.

She saw that she was in a large and beautifully decorated room with brocade covered walls on which were hung some very attractive pictures.

When she looked up she could see that the ceiling was painted with goddesses and cupids.

She was lying in a bed that was surmounted by a gold corona and the curtains which fell from it were of lace and silk.

She knew the answer to the question, but she had to ask it.

"Where ... am I?"

"You are, *Madame*, in the house of the *Duc* de Saverne," the Nun replied. "It is where you were on the night of the Ball."

Lina drew in her breath.

The night when the *Comtesse* had shot her, the night when the *Duc* had said goodbye and told her he would never see her again.

There was one more question she wanted to ask, one question that trembled on her lips, but she could not ask it because she thought she could not bear to hear the answer.

It was quite simple: Had the *Duc* gone? Had he left Paris?

If he had, she knew it meant that she would never see him again.

Then she remembered she had saved his life.

If she had not thrown herself in front of him the *Comtesse* would have killed him as she intended to do, for she had been pointing the revolver at his heart.

Lina thought of all that had happened. Then it was

too much for her to contemplate, too much to think about. She shut her eyes and tried to sleep.

"Look at your lovely flowers, *Madame*," the Nun said as she came into the room carrying a vase filled with orchids.

The speaker was the other of the two Nuns who were looking after Lina. She was younger and obviously enjoyed the material things of life more than her elderly companion.

"They are beautiful!" Lina exclaimed.

"Every day *Monsieur le Duc* seems to find something new to send you, *Madame*. Soon we will have nowhere to put the flowers."

It was true. The bedroom was beginning to look like a bower and made Lina think of the arbour in which the *Duc* had kissed her.

In the last few days when she had been growing stronger and able to think sensibly and clearly, she had been acutely conscious that the *Duc* was thinking of her as she was thinking of him.

She could almost feel her vibrations linking with his and she thought now that even before she had realised this the flowers reminded her of him.

She thought of him downstairs, moving about the exquisitely furnished rooms, and she hoped perhaps he would send her a note or a message, but only the flowers arrived and she wanted to think that they spoke to her without words.

161

At the same time she could not help worrying about what was happening.

She supposed, although she did not like to ask the Nuns, that Kitty, Daisy, and Evie had gone back to England.

If not, they had not come to see her, nor had they communicated with her.

The Surgeon had said specifically, according to the Nuns, that she was to have complete rest and quiet, and it was in fact only yesterday that she had begun to feel like herself.

Today, despite the fact that her arm hurt when she moved it, and it throbbed when she tried to sleep, she felt almost normal.

When they dressed it she could not bear to look at the ugly wound which was just below her shoulder and seemed to disfigure her body.

The Surgeon had called this morning and said as if he sensed what she was feeling:

"I am very proud that you are such a good patient, *Madame*. In a year's time you will hardly know that this has ever happened to you."

"Surely it will...leave a...terrible scar?" Lina enquired.

The Surgeon smiled.

"I cannot promise there will be no scar, but it will be little more than a white line on your arm, and the place will always be concealed by the sleeve of your gown, even when you are wearing evening-dress."

"Are you...sure of...that?" Lina asked.

"I promise you I am speaking the truth," the Surgeon

replied, "and as I have said, you are an example of my skill of which I am very proud."

Because he was a Frenchman he made what he was saying sound as if he was flirting with her and Lina said impulsively:

"Thank you... thank you, *Monsieur*. I was... afraid I would be... disfigured for... life!"

"You will be just as beautiful as you have ever been," the Surgeon replied.

When he left he raised her hand to his lips and said:

"*Merci, Madame,* for being such an exemplary patient, and the loveliest person on whom I have ever operated!"

His compliment made Lina blush, but she was wondering when he left whether the *Duc* would think the same.

Then for the first time with a sense of shock she remembered that before Kitty had left she would have told the *Duc* the truth about her.

However ill or wounded she might be it would not have prevented Kitty, Daisy, and Evie from taking their revenge on the *Duc* which they had planned so carefully.

As if she wanted confirmation of this the Nun brought a letter and set it down on the bed in front of her.

"I was told to give you this, *Madame*," she said, "when you were better, and as *Monsieur le Medecin* is so pleased with you, I expect you would like to read it."

Because it was a letter, for a moment Lina's heart

leaped and she thought perhaps it was from the one person that she wished to hear from.

Then she knew as she saw the hand-writing who had written to her.

"Will you . . . open it . . . please?" she asked the Nun and her voice trembled.

The Nun slit open the envelope and drew something out.

Lina had one look at it and knew that it was the cheque which Kitty had promised her if she played her part competently in the role they had assigned to her.

Because she did not speak, the Nun realising that what she was holding out to Lina was a cheque and not a letter said:

"I will put this in a drawer of your dressing-table, *Madame*, so it will be there when you are up and about."

She walked across the room as she spoke, took up a tray on which there were some glasses which had been used and went from the room.

Lina leaned back against her pillows thinking.

It was difficult to force herself to face the truth, but it was something that had to be done.

Kitty had sent her the cheque, which meant that her association with The Three Beauties was finished and when she returned to London she would have to look for other employment.

If she cashed the cheque she could, it was true, live for a long time without having to work.

At the same time every instinct in her body made her wish to tear it up.

Of one thing she was quite certain: the *Duc*, although he would obviously be kind because she had saved his life, would have no wish to be involved with her in the future.

Her face burned with embarrassment as she thought of Kitty's triumph when she told him how easily they had deceived him, and that his attentions had been expended on a farmer's daughter whom they had dolled up to make a fool of him.

She could imagine how Kitty would have gloried in her revenge and Daisy and Evie would have been there too hoping what was said would not only humiliate but hurt the *Duc*.

'I should...not have...let it...happen,' Lina thought, 'I should have told him the...truth about the plot and who I...really...am.'

Then it seemed as if whatever she told him, whatever she revealed would have only spoiled and damaged their love.

With a little cry she felt that without meaning to she had destroyed something as perfect and yet at the same time as fragile as the orchids he had just sent her.

"I should...never have...come to Paris in the...first place!" she accused herself.

Then she knew that whatever happened she would never regret having met the most wonderful man in the world and known that for a very short while he had loved her as she loved him.

Now he must be thinking of her as a liar, a woman who had set out to deceive him by pretending to be married. A woman who in his idealism he had been prepared to leave and never see again because he believed her, as he had said, 'essentially pure and innocent.'

Now she understood why he had not written her a note or tried to see her.

He might have sent her flowers, but those were just an expression of his gratitude because she had saved him from the bullet of a woman who was mad.

She had been unable to think sensibly and had been deluding herself when she had thought she could feel his vibrations.

What he would be feeling for her now was contempt and, what was more, she had put him in the embarrassing position of having no answer to the taunts and jeers of the women who had wished to revenge themselves on him.

Left alone in the beautiful room Lina went down into a little hell of her own and she wished she could either die or run away and hide where nobody could find her.

For a moment she planned how she would creep out of the house and disappear. Then she knew it would be an impossible thing to do even if her legs were strong enough to carry her.

"What...shall I do? What shall I...do?" she asked.

Then as she wanted to cry at her own helplessness she thought perhaps there was no need for her to do anything.

After what had happened the *Duc* would not want to see her, and therefore when she was well enough he would make arrangements for her to travel back to England and they would never meet again.

Now that he knew the truth, he would not, as he had said, think about her, dream about her, and keep her in his heart for ever.

It was a worse agony than anything she had experienced before to know that she had disillusioned him, and Lina felt the tears flooding into her eyes and running slowly down her cheeks.

She heard the door open and thinking it was one of the Nuns she felt hastily under her pillow for a handkerchief, but she could not find it.

Then as she groped with her eyes shut hoping perhaps the Nun would not notice the tears, a deep voice asked:

"You are not crying, Lina?"

She felt her heart leap and turn a dozen somersaults.

As she opened her eyes because he was there the room seemed to be brilliant with a celestial light and it seemed so dazzling that it blinded her.

The *Duc* stood looking at her for a moment, then he took a handkerchief from his breast-pocket and very gently wiped the tears from her cheeks.

She trembled because he was touching her and she wanted to speak, but no words could pass her lips.

The *Duc* having wiped away her tears sat down very gently on the side of the mattress facing her.

He looked at her for a long moment before he said:

"I have not been allowed to come and see you until now. The Surgeon has told me how pleased he is with you, so I did not expect to find you in tears."

167

"I . . . I am . . . sorry."

"It is I who should say that, not you," the *Duc* said. "You are not in pain?"

"No . . . no! My arm is . . . better."

"So I have been told and if this has hurt you, I assure you I have suffered excruciatingly knowing it was my fault that you were injured in such a crazy manner."

It was difficult for Lina to listen to what he was saying. All she knew was that it was wonderful that he was there beside her and she could see him and know that he had not left.

'I must remember . . . everything he says,' she thought frantically. 'Perhaps in a . . . moment he will say . . . goodbye, . . . but at least I have . . . seen him . . . . . . again.'

She thought she had forgotten how attractive he was, how different from any other man, and the look in his eyes made her feel strange sensations pulsating through her.

It was impossible to describe in words but all she knew was that she loved him so overwhelmingly and completely that it was difficult not to tell him so, though she knew it was something he would not want to hear.

The *Duc* was still looking at her, and Lina was conscious that she must appear totally different from any way he had seen her before.

The young Nun had parted her hair in the middle and drawn it down on either side of her face to tie it

168

with bows of pale blue ribbon so that it fell down over her breasts.

Lina felt that while she was neat and tidy she must look absurdly childlike.

As the *Duc's* eyes seemed to be searching her face penetratingly, she felt shy and her eye-lashes were dark against her pale cheeks because she dare not look at him any longer.

"How can you have been so brave, so incredibly brave," he asked, "as to save my life at the risk of your own?"

"I . . . I did not . . . think about it," Lina answered. "I just . . . wanted to save you."

"Why?"

The answer was obvious, but Lina felt she must not say it.

There was a moment's pause. Then he said:

"You saved me because you love me, and now, my darling, I have learnt that there is nothing to stop me from telling you of my love, and asking you how soon you will marry me."

Lina looked up at him in astonishment, feeling that she could not have heard him aright.

"D–did you . . . ask me to . . . m–marry you?" she whispered.

The *Duc* smiled.

"I do not think I ever really believed in that elderly husband who was not interested in you and spent his time fishing. No man, unless he was blind, deaf, and an imbecile would have allowed you to go to Paris

169

without being there to protect you from men like me!"

There was a note of amusement in his voice, and as he spoke he looked so happy that it seemed in some way as if he was younger than he had ever seemed before.

Lina could only stare at him and after a moment she managed to say:

"What . . . else did . . . Kitty tell you?"

"Is it important?"

"I want . . . to know."

"She told me how she, Daisy and Evie had planned their little act of revenge, and thought because you were so beautiful that I would find you irresistible— which I did!"

Lina drew in her breath.

"They wanted to . . . humiliate . . . you."

"They made that very clear," the *Duc* said, still with a note of amusement in his voice. "I have always prided myself on my instinct in knowing exactly what a person is like, without having to read references or a dossier and they were delighted to demonstrate that in this instance I was wrong."

Lina made a little murmur. Then she said in a voice that did not sound like her own:

"Although I . . . accepted money to . . . deceive you . . . you still ask me to be your . . . wife?"

"What else do you expect me to do?" the *Duc* enquired.

He saw Lina stiffen, and he knew it had flashed into her mind that he was asking her simply out of gratitude because she had saved him.

He smiled, and it made him look even more attractive.

"You are not really so foolish as to think that?" he asked. "If what I felt for you, my darling, was no more than gratitude, I could give you a cheque for a very large amount of money, at which I value myself in hard cash, and send you back to England!"

His voice deepened and he went on:

"But you know what we feel for each other, and I am not at all interested in where you were born or what your parents are like, but just you."

Lina drew in her breath and felt as if once again the room was filled with celestial light.

She did not have to remember the conversation she had had with his grandmother to know what his family expected of him, or what indeed any Frenchman in his position would want as the background of the woman he married.

But thinking, as Kitty would have told him, that she was no more than the daughter of a farmer who was prepared to accept the job of a lady's-maid, nevertheless he, the *Duc* himself, had said that it was impossible to put her feelings into words.

Lina put out her hand as if she must touch him to know that he was real, and she said in a little incoherent voice:

"I...I cannot...believe it...I think I am... dreaming...or still...unconscious."

"I will prove to you that you are awake," the *Duc* said. "But my lovely one, we must wait until you are well enough before I can make you mine! Yet, thank God we can be together, and there are no more foolish barriers between us."

Before Lina could answer he went on:

"When I said you were pure and innocent I was not wrong, and I knew when I kissed you that you had never been kissed before."

His eyes searched hers before he asked:

"That is true? I was the first man to do so?"

"Yes... yes!" Lina replied, "but there is... something I must... tell you."

"There are a great many things we have to tell each other," the *Duc* said, "but, my precious, I must not tire you now. I promised the Nuns I would only stay for a few minutes, and already I have broken my promise. So I am going to leave you, but I will come back later in the afternoon."

"No, no! Please...!" Lina began, but it was no use.

The *Duc* bent forward and his lips were on hers.

It was a very gentle kiss such as he might have given a child, but to Lina it was all the wonder and the glory that she had felt before and once again she felt as if he was taking her to a special Heaven that belonged only to them.

Then as her lips quivered beneath his he rose, kissed her hand, then before she could speak, before she could even tell him how much she loved him, he had gone from the room and she was alone.

She leant back against the pillows thinking it could not be true and that she must have dreamed that the

Duc, believing what Kitty had told him, had asked her to be his wife.

She knew then that just as her love for him had been great enough to risk her life for his, so his love for her was great enough for him to marry her despite the fact that it would be breaking every tradition in which he had been brought up.

"I love him! I love him!" Lina told herself. "Oh, God, how can I ever thank You for...letting us find...each other?"

———————————

After luncheon Lina slept for two hours, dreaming that the *Duc*'s lips were against hers and his arms were around her.

When she awoke the younger Nun placed a chiffon and lace shawl over her shoulders, which hid her bandages.

"Where did this come from?" Lina asked. "It is not mine."

"*Monsieur le Duc* gave it to me for you," she replied. "I think he understood that you would not wish to show your bandages."

Lina smiled. She could not believe any man could be so considerate or so understanding.

The Nun brushed her hair and arranged it not on the sides of her cheeks which Lina felt made her look too childlike, but swept it back and tied it with a bow at the base of her neck.

"You look like one of the Saints or perhaps an Angel in our Chapel," the Nun said admiringly.

"Thank you," Lina replied.

The blinds were raised a little to let in more of the sun, and sitting up against the pillows with the *Duc*'s monogram on them, in the beautiful bedroom with the painted cupids on the ceiling overhead, Lina felt as if she was enveloped by love.

Because she thought it would please him, she asked the Nun at the last moment to bring her the diamond star which the *Duc* had given her and which she learned had been brought with her belongings from the *Comtesse*'s house.

"There are some pieces of jewellery which came with your gowns," the Nun had said, "and I have put them in a drawer of the dressing-table, *Madame*, so that they will be safe."

Lina had thought they were her mother's jewels that she had brought with her to Paris, then she remembered on the night of the Ball she had received the diamond star.

The Nun pinned it for her on top of the chiffon wrap and Lina saw the *Duc*'s eyes on it as he came towards her.

He took her hand in his and said:

"So my Star is no longer out of reach."

Lina's fingers trembled as she replied:

"Not...unless you wish it...to be."

"I want to touch it and hold it for ever."

He looked at her before he added:

"When I saw you this morning, I thought it impossible for any woman to be more beautiful, and yet when I look at you now you are infinitely lovelier than

174

you were then. What have you done to me, Lina, to make me feel like this?"

"Like . . . what?"

It was difficult to speak because from the moment he had come into the room she had felt such strange sensations sweep through her.

She could only look at him, her eyes very wide, feeling that her love poured out towards him and he must know how much she adored him.

The *Duc* sat down on the side of the bed as he had that morning, and kissed her fingers, one by one before his lips touched her palm.

Then as he felt the thrill that went through her because his mouth was insistent, demanding, he laughed softly and bent forward to kiss her lips.

She felt as he did so that they were so close, so attuned to each other that there was no need for explanations or words.

They were one and not even the Sacrament of Marriage would make them closer.

"I . . . love . . . you!"

"As I love you," the *Duc* answered, "and ever since I saw you this morning I have been thanking God because I have been allowed to find you."

"That is what . . . I have been doing . . . too," Lina whispered.

"But of course," the *Duc* smiled, "I knew that."

He sat back a little but still held her hand close in his.

"What I am going to say to you, my darling, is that although it is difficult to explain, I have instinctively

175

always been looking for you, only, until I found you, to be disappointed."

Lina knew he was speaking of the other women to whom he had made love and with whom while they had loved him he had always become bored and left them as he had left Daisy, Evie, and Kitty.

"Please . . . you do not . . . have to . . . explain."

"I know that," the *Duc* replied, "but because there may be people who will try to hurt you by speaking of my reputation and perhaps implying that I have been in love before, I want to make absolutely sure you understand that what I feel for you is different, so different that only you can understand why that is the truth."

"I . . . I do . . . understand."

"It has been a long, long pilgrimage," he went on, "which I thought at times would never end. Now it is over. I have found the Shangri-La which all men seek, and I have been blessed, as I do not deserve to be, by your love."

Lina gave a little cry of happiness.

"How can you say such . . . wonderful things to me?"

"I want to say them and go on saying them."

"I have . . . something to tell you which is very . . . important."

"I am waiting to hear it," he answered, "but first I want to kiss you."

Lina took her hand from his and put it against his chest to hold him away from her.

"You kissed me this morning," she said, "until I

could think of nothing except our love. Please... listen to me now."

"I can think of nothing more interesting or important than that I should kiss you," the *Duc* said. "However if it will please you, I will listen to what you have to say. But hurry, my darling, for it is an agony to sit here when you look so alluring and so inviting that words I assure you, are quite superfluous."

"Not the... ones I have to... say," Lina persisted.

"I am listening."

His eyes as he spoke were on her lips and because he was so near, because he excited her so tremendously, it was very hard to concentrate.

"I... think," she managed to begin at last, "when Kitty told you I had applied for the... position of her lady's-maid because I could speak French... she said I had just come from the... country... and I had not held such a position before."

There was a pause while Lina knew that the *Duc* was finding it hard because he was thinking of her, to remember exactly what Kitty had said.

"That is what she told me," he agreed at last, "although I was not particularly interested in your past."

"Did she tell you what my name was before she invented one for me?"

"Now—let me see—" the *Duc* replied almost as if he was humouring a child. "I think, yes, I am sure, she said your name was Cromer, a rather dull name for somebody so beautiful. I shall be glad when you change it to mine."

"Cromer was the name of... one of my...

177

Governesses," Lina said. "My real name is...Lina Cressington-Combe."

"Cressington-Combe?" the *Duc* repeated. "I have heard that name before. In fact it is a strange coincidence but when I was at Oxford, on the wall opposite to the place where I sat in the Hall was a portrait labelled: *'George Frederick Cressington-Combe, 4th Earl of Wallingham.'* Was he a relation?"

"My...grandfather!"

The *Duc* stared at her. Then he said:

"I do not understand."

"My father is the present Earl, but I ran away from home."

"Why?"

"Because Papa wanted me to marry a horrible, elderly man whose real interest in me was that if I became his wife he thought he would be accepted...socially in the County."

"Thank God you ran away!" the *Duc* exclaimed. "At the same time, my darling, how could you take such risks as to go to London and be prepared to take a job as a servant?"

"I originally applied for a post as Governess both because I had to earn money, and also because I thought it would be a clever way to hide," Lina explained. "But when I went to the Domestic Bureau I learned that Lady Birchington required a lady's-maid who could speak French."

"I can hardly believe it!"

"I am...ashamed that I should have been so...deceitful, but when they offered me so much money . . . £200 . . . I knew it would be stupid to refuse . . . I was also tempted to accept because I so much wanted to . . . see Paris."

"I can understand," the *Duc* said, "at the same time you will never, my precious, beautiful little Star, take such risks with yourself again, or be put in such an invidious position."

He spoke insistently, then suddenly he laughed.

"So Kitty's revenge was pointless after all," he said, "for obviously you are everything I believed you to be, only more so."

"It was . . . wrong of me to . . . act such a . . . role," Lina said unhappily. "I am . . . ashamed now that I . . . took any part in it."

"There is no need to be," the *Duc* said. "All that matters, my darling one, is that we found each other, and although I would make you my wife even if you were the daughter of a crossing-sweeper, it will certainly please my family that your father is an English nobleman."

"I am afraid your . . . grandmother will still think I am not . . . good enough for you," Lina said hesitatingly.

The *Duc* laughed again.

"*Grand'mere* who by the way is staying in the house so that you are conventionally chaperoned is at the moment so grateful that you saved my life that when you are well enough to see her she will not only thank you profusely, but welcome you warmly as my wife."

"I must . . . ask," Lina said, "what . . . happened to the . . . *Comtesse*?"

179

She could hardly bear to say the words because once again she could hear the *Comtesse's* mad voice and feel the horror which had swept through her when she saw the revolver pointed at the *Duc's* heart.

"I blame myself that you should have suffered at her hands," the *Duc* said quietly. "She has always been a little unbalanced. In fact when her husband died a year after their marriage it was agreed in the family that because she was not entirely normal no effort should be made to find her another husband."

He paused before he went on:

"When she grew older she seemed to become a little better, except where I was concerned. It became an obsession with her that she would marry me, which was of course, something that I would never have considered, nor have I ever, and this is the truth, my darling, paid her any attention."

The *Duc* searched Lina's face as if he wanted to be sure that she believed him and when he knew that she did he continued:

"But I knew, as the rest of the family did not, that Yvonne was becoming more and more determined that I should be her husband, and when we were alone she became violent and often hysterical."

"How . . . terrible for . . . you!" Lina murmured.

"I was beginning to realise that something would have to be done about it," the *Duc* said. "Then when she took some interest in the Ball I was arranging, I thought it might perhaps help her and therefore agreed that she should give a large dinner-party as other members of my family were giving."

180

"But you arranged for Kitty to...stay with her?" Lina asked, remembering what the *Comtesse* had said about Kitty to her.

"That was a mistake made by my grandmother," the *Duc* answered. "She did not know what Yvonne was really like so she arranged it when I was not in Paris and when I returned the letter of invitation had already been sent to London."

"So you...thought it...best to leave things as they...were," Lina murmured.

"Very foolishly," the *Duc* said, "or perhaps, like most men, I was avoiding a scene."

He sighed before he went on:

"Perhaps the sins of omission are the ones for which we are most severely punished, and on this occasion, because I was so foolish, I might have lost you."

There was a note in his voice which told Lina how deeply he felt over what had occurred, but because it no longer seemed to matter she asked:

"You are sure...quite sure you...want to marry me?"

"I am sure! Quite sure I intend to do so," the *Duc* answered, "and nothing and nobody shall stop me!"

"Our marriage will be...the most...wonderful thing that...ever happened to...me."

"And wonderful for me too and it is going to take me a lifetime to explain to you how fortunate I am and how much I worship and adore you."

He moved a little nearer to her as he said:

"Now may I kiss Lady Lina Cressington-Combe?"

Lina gave a little laugh and he said:

"No, that is not right. I am kissing a Star that was out of reach. A Star that I believed was unobtainable and must be left twinkling far away in the sky because it was so perfect that I must not spoil it."

"Now... I am no... longer in the... sky... but here... with you."

There was a little note of passion in Lina's voice that the *Duc* did not miss.

He put his arm around her very gently, so as not to jar her arm, but his lips when they found hers were fierce, demanding and passionate.

She knew as he kissed her that this was the burning fire of love of which he had spoken.

She felt it sweep through her, rising from the very depths of her body up through her breasts and into her lips to meet the fire in him.

It was love as he had described it, a love so omnipotent, overwhelming, and irresistible that neither of them had any defence against it.

It was a love which swept them enveloped in a celestial light into a Heaven which was theirs for all eternity.

ABOUT THE AUTHOR

Barbara Cartland, the world's most famous romantic novelist, who is also an historian, playwright, lecturer, political speaker and television personality, has now written over 300 books and sold 200 million books over the world.

She has also had many historical works published and has written four autobiographies as well as the biographies of her mother and that of her brother, Ronald Cartland, who was the first Member of Parliament to be killed in the last war. This book has a preface by Sir Winston Churchill and has just been republished with an introduction by Sir Arthur Bryant.

LOVE AT THE HELM, a novel written with the help and inspiration of the late Admiral of the Fleet, the Earl Mountbatten of Burma, is being sold for the Mountbatten Memorial Trust.

Miss Cartland in 1978 sang an Album of Love Songs with the Royal Philharmonic Orchestra.

In 1976 by writing twenty-one books, she broke the world record and has continued for the following four years with twenty-four, twenty, twenty-three and twenty-four. She is in the GUINNESS BOOK OF RECORDS as the best selling author alive.

She is unique in that she was one and two in the Dalton List of Best Sellers, and one week had four books in the top twenty.

In private life Barbara Cartland, who is a Dame of the Order of St. John of Jerusalem, Chairman of the St. John Council in Hertfordshire and Deputy President of the St. John Ambulance Brigade, has also fought for better conditions and salaries for Midwives and Nurses.

Barbara Cartland is deeply interested in Vitamin Therapy and is President of the British National Association for Health. Her book THE MAGIC OF HONEY has sold throughout the world and is translated into many languages. She has a magazine, BARBARA CARTLAND'S WORLD OF ROMANCE, now being published in the U. S. A. The World of Oz travel bureau is doing BARBARA CARTLAND'S ROMANTIC TOURS in conjunction with BRITISH AIRWAYS.